THE CAMPFIRE GIRLS
SERIES

ᐷ

A CAMPFIRE GIRL'S FIRST COUNCIL FIRE

A CAMPFIRE GIRL'S CHUM

A CAMPFIRE GIRL IN SUMMER CAMP

A CAMPFIRE GIRL'S ADVENTURE

A CAMPFIRE GIRL'S TEST OF FRIENDSHIP

A CAMPFIRE GIRL'S HAPPINESS

She turned—and looked up into the evil eyes of
Farmer Weeks.

A Campfire Girl's Chum

By
JANE L. STEWART

CAMPFIRE GIRLS SERIES
VOLUME II

WILDSIDE PRESS

The Camp Fire Girls On the Farm

CHAPTER I

IN THE CITY

"I never dreamed of such a lovely room, Zara, did you?"

Bessie King, her eyes open with admiration and wonder, asked her chum the question in a room in the home of Eleanor Mercer, Guardian of the Manasquan Camp Fire, of the Camp Fire Girls. Both the girls were new members of the organization, and Bessie, who had lived all her life in the country, and had known nothing of the luxuries and comforts that girls in the city, or the luckier ones of them, at least, take almost as a matter of course, had found something new to astonish her in almost every hour since they had come to the city.

"I've dreamed of it—yes," said Zara. "You see I've been in the city before, Bessie; and I've seen houses like this, and I've guessed that the rooms inside must be something like this, though I never lived in one. It's beautiful."

"I almost wish we were going to stay here, Zara. But I suppose it will be nice when we go to the farm."

Eleanor Mercer, who had been standing for a moment in the doorway, came in then, laughing merrily. She had overheard the remark, and Bessie was greatly distressed when she discovered it.

"Oh, Miss Eleanor!" she exclaimed. "Please, please don't think I'm ungrateful. I want to do whatever you think is right—"

"I know that, Bessie, and I know just what you were thinking, too. Well, you're going to have a surprise—I can promise you that. This farm isn't a bit like the farm you know about. I guess you know too much about one sort of farm to want ever to see another, don't you?"

"Maybe there are different sorts of farms,"

admitted Bessie. "I don't like Paw Hoover's kind."

Eleanor laughed again. She was a fresh, bright-cheeked girl, not so many years older than Bessie herself. One might guess, indeed, that she, as Guardian of her Camp Fire, didn't much more than manage to fulfill the requirement that Guardians, like Scoutmasters among the Boy Scouts, must be over twenty-one years of age.

"Indeed there are different sorts of farms from that one, Bessie," she said. "You'll see a farm where everything is done the way it should be, and, while I think Paw Hoover's a mighty nice man, I've got an idea that on his farm everything is done just about opposite to the proper fashion."

"When are we going, Miss Eleanor?"

Zara asked that question. In the last few days a hunted look had left Zara's eyes, for with relief from certain worries she had begun to be happier, and she was always asking questions now.

"I don't know exactly, Zara, but not right away.

We want all the girls to go out together. We're
going to have our next Council Fire at the farm.
And some of them can't get away just now. But
it will be fairly soon, I can promise you that. You
like the country, don't you, Zara?"

"Indeed I do, Miss Eleanor! Until they took
my father away I was ever so happy there."

"And just think, you're going to see him to-
morrow, Zara! He's well, and as soon as he heard
that you were here and safe, he stopped worrying. That was his chief trouble—he seemed to
think more about what would happen to you than
that he was in trouble himself."

"I knew he'd be thinking about me," said Zara.
"He always did, even when he had most to bother
him."

"I was sure he was a good father, Zara, when
I heard you talk about him—and I've been surer
of it than ever since I've had a chance to find out
about him. My cousin, who's a lawyer, you know,
is going to see that he is properly treated, and
he says that Mr. Weeks, who tried so hard to

make you stay behind and work for him, is at the bottom of all the trouble.''

Zara shuddered at the name.

''How I hate that Farmer Weeks!'' she exclaimed.

Eleanor Mercer sighed and shook her head. She couldn't blame Zara for hating the man, and yet, as she well knew, the spirit in the little foreign girl that cherished hatred and ideas of revenge was bad—bad for her. But how to eradicate it, and to make Zara feel more charitable, was something that puzzled the Guardian mightily, and was, as she foresaw, likely to puzzle her still more. She left the two girls together, then, to answer a call from outside the room.

''I don't exactly *like* Farmer Weeks myself,'' said Bessie, thoughtfully, when they were alone. ''But what's the use of hating him, Zara?''

''Why, Bessie! He made us run away from Hedgeville—he made me, anyhow. And if he'd had his way, he'd have taken me back, and had me bound over to work for him just for board until I was twenty-one, if I hadn't starved to death first. You know what a miser he is.''

"Yes, that's true enough, Zara. But, after all, if it hadn't happened that way, we'd never have met Miss Eleanor and the Camp Fire Girls, would we? And you're not sorry for that, are you?''

Zara's face, which had grown hard, softened.

"No, indeed, Bessie! They're the nicest people I ever did know, except you. But, even after we were with them, and had started to come to the city with them, he caught me, and if it hadn't been for you following us and guessing where he'd put me, I'd be with him now.''

"Well, you're not, Zara. And you want to try to think of the good things that happen. Then you won't have time to remember all the bad things, and they won't bother you any more than if they'd never happened at all. Don't you see?''

"Well, I'll try, Bessie. I guess they can't hurt us here, anyhow, or on the farm. I think we're going to have lots of fun on the farm.''

"I hope so, Zara. But I've often read about

how jolly farms are—in books. In the books, you don't have to get up at four o'clock on the cold winter mornings to do chores, and you don't have to work all the time, the way I had to do for Maw Hoover.''

''I guess that was just because it was Maw Hoover, Bessie, and not because it was on a farm. She'd have been mean to you, and made you work all the time, just the same, if it had been a farm or wherever it was. I think it's people that make you happy or unhappy, not other things.''

''I guess that's about right, Zara. I'm awfully glad you're going to see your father in the morning. I bet he'll be glad to see you.''

''Bessie! Zara!'' Miss Eleanor was calling from downstairs, and they ran to answer the call.

''Come into the parlor,'' she said, as she heard them approaching.

They obeyed, and found her talking to a tall, good looking young man, who smiled cheerfully at them.

''This is my cousin, Charlie Jamieson, the law-

2—C2

yer, girls,'' said Miss Eleanor. "I've told him
all about you, of course, and now he wants to talk
to you.''

"I'm going to be your lawyer, you know,"
Charlie Jamieson explained. "Girls like you
don't have much use for a lawyer, as a rule, but
I guess you need one about as badly as anyone
I can think of. So I'm going to take the job,
unless you know someone better.''

"No, indeed," they chorused in answer, and
both laughed when they saw that he was joking.

"I wish about a thousand other people were
as anxious as that to be my clients. Then maybe
I'd make enough money to pay my office rent.''

"Don't you believe him, girls," said Eleanor,
laughing, too. "He's one of the smartest young
lawyers in this town, and he's busy most of the
time, too. He always is, lately, when I want him
to come to one of my parties or anything like
that.''

"Well, let's be serious for a while," said
Jamieson. "I'm going to try to help your father

out of his trouble, Zara, and I'm finding it pretty hard, because he doesn't want to trust me, or tell me much of anything. Perhaps you'll be able to do better."

Zara looked grave.

"I don't know much," she said. "But I do know this. My father used to trust people, but they've treated him so badly that he's afraid to do it any more. Like Farmer Weeks—I think he trusted him."

"That's more than I'd do," said the lawyer, with a grin. "From all I've heard of him I wouldn't trust him around the corner with a counterfeit nickel—if I wanted it back. And—well, that sort of helps to get us started, doesn't it? You know why your father's in trouble? It's because they say he's been making bad money at that little house where you lived in Hedgeville."

"He didn't!" said Zara. "I know he didn't!"

"Well, the district attorney—he's the one who has to be against your father, you know—says that everyone in Hedgeville seems to think he did,

And he says that where there's so much smoke there must be some fire; that if so many people think your father was crooked, they must be right. I told him that was unfair, but he just laughed at me.''

"You may have to be a witness, Zara," said Eleanor.

"A witness?" said Zara, puzzled.

"Yes. You may have to go to court, and tell them what you know. They'll ask you questions, though, and you'll just have to answer them, and tell the truth just as you know it.''

"Yes, that's why I'm here," said Jamieson, nodding his head. "You see, I may need you very badly and I want to make sure that they can't take you back to Hedgeville. You never saw anyone who told you that as long as your father couldn't look after you any more, you would have to stay with this Weeks, did you? A judge, I mean?"

"No. But when Farmer Weeks caught me that time, and carried me away in his buggy, he said he was going to take me to Zebulon—that's the county seat, you know—and have everything fixed up. But Bessie got me away from him before that could happen, so it was all right.''

"And when he came after you at Pine Bridge—after you'd crossed the line into this state—the policeman there wouldn't let him touch you, would he?''

"No. Farmer Weeks showed him a paper, with a big red seal on it, but the policeman said it was no good in this state.''

"That sounds all right. I guess they can't touch you. I had to make sure of that, you see. But, young lady, you want to be mighty careful. If they can get you over the state line, no matter how, they've got you. And I shouldn't be surprised if they tried just to kidnap you.''

Eleanor Mercer looked frightened.

"Do you think there's really any danger, Charlie?'' she asked.

"I certainly do. And it's because I don't know just what it is they're after. There's something

funny here, something we don't know about at
all, yet. Maybe her father could tell us, but he
isn't ready to do it. And I don't blame him
much. I guess, from all I've heard, that he's
had about as bad a time here with spies and
enemies as he could have had anywhere in Europe.''

"You hear that, Zara? You must be very careful. Don't go out alone, and if anyone tries to
speak to you, no matter what they tell you, you
pay no attention to them. If they keep on bothering you, speak to a policeman, if there's one
around, and say that you want him to stop them
from bothering you.''

"Good idea,'' said Charlie Jamieson. "And if
you do have to speak to a policeman, you mention
my name. They all know me, and I guess most
of them like me well enough to do any little favor
for a friend of mine.''

Then Jamieson turned to Bessie.

"We've got to think about your case, too,'' he
said. "Miss Mercer tells me that you don't know

what's become of your father and mother. Just
what do you know about them?''

"Not very much," said Bessie, bravely, although the disappearance of her parents always
weighed heavily on her mind. "When I was a
little bit of a girl they left me with the Hoovers,
at Hedgeville, and I lived with them after that.
Maw Hoover said they promised to come back
for me, and to pay her board for looking after
me until they came, and that they did pay the
board for a while. But then they stopped writing
altogether, and no one has heard from them for
years."

"H'm! Where did the last letter they wrote
come from?"

"San Francisco. I've heard Maw Hoover say
that, often. But that was years and years ago."

"Well, that's better than nothing, anyhow.
You see, the Hoovers wouldn't have known how
to start looking for them, even if they'd been
particularly anxious to do it."

"And I don't believe they were," said Eleanor

Mercer, indignantly. "They treated her shamefully, Charlie—made her work like a hired girl, and never paid her for it, at all. Instead, they acted, or the woman did, anyhow, just as if they were giving her charity in letting her stay there. Wasn't that an outrage?"

"Lots of people act as if they were being charitable when they get a good deal more than they give," said the lawyer dryly.

"Maw Hoover was always calling me lazy, and saying she'd send me to the poor-farm," said Bessie. "But it was she and Jake that made things so hard. Paw Hoover was always good to me, and he helped me to get away, too."

"That's what I'm driving at," said Jamieson. "You had a right to go whenever you liked, if they hadn't adopted you, or anything like that. Really, all you were in their place was a servant who wasn't getting paid."

"I knew she had a right to go," said Eleanor. "That's why I helped her, of course."

"Then we're all right. If she'd really run

away from someone who had a right to keep her, it would be harder. I might be able to prove that they weren't fit guardians, but that's always hard, and it's a good thing we don't need to do it. Hullo, what's the matter now?"

"Look!" said Zara, who had risen, and was looking keenly at a figure across the street. "See, Bessie, don't you know who that is, even in those clothes?"

Bessie followed her eyes, and started to her feet.

"It's Jake Hoover!" she cried. "What can he want here?"

CHAPTER II

Startled and frightened by Bessie's cry, Eleanor jumped up and followed her to the window.

"Well," said Eleanor, "I never saw him before, but I can't say I'm sorry for that. He looks mean enough to do all the things you've told us about him, Bessie."

"Who is this Hoover? One of the people Bessie lived with in Hedgeville?" asked Jamieson.

"Yes; he's the son of the old farmer and his wife."

"H'm!" said the lawyer. "Then evidently he knows where she has come. That looks bad."

"Yes. You see, he was always his mother's pet," said Eleanor, "and I suppose he'll tell her all about the girls."

"Let him! I guess it can't do any harm. I don't see how it can now, anyhow, unless he's in

with this Weeks or someone we don't know anything about, who has some interest in this affair.
That's one of the things that's going to give me
trouble, I'm afraid.''

"What do you mean, Charlie?"

"Just that there's so much I don't know. You
see, there's something mighty queer loose here.
I can see that. There's a mystery and we haven't
the key. The chances are that the people we've
got to fight know everything there is to be known,
while we don't even know who they are, except
this Weeks. And I'm not a bit sure about him.''

"I am, Charlie. If you'd seen him, and heard
all about the way he acted, you'd know he was
an enemy all right.''

"That's not just what I mean, Eleanor. I'm
thinking that perhaps he isn't just making this
fight on his own account; that maybe he's working
for someone else.''

"I hadn't thought of that at all—"

"No reason why you should! But it's my business to think of every little thing that may hap-

pen to have an influence on any case that I'm
mixed up in, you see. And, as I understand it,
this Weeks is pretty close—pretty fond of money,
isn't he?''

"He's a regular old miser, that's what he is!"
said Zara, her eyes flashing.

"There's a motive for him, you see. Someone
might have a reason for wanting to keep Zara
where they could get her easily, and if they offered
Weeks a little money to get hold of her, I judge
he'd do it fast enough.''

"But why shouldn't they try to get hold of
her themselves, if that's what they want?"

"There might be lots of reasons for that. They
might want to keep out of it, so that no one would
know they were doing it, you see. That would
be one reason. And then this Weeks is a bit of
a politician. He's got a good, strong pull in that
county, I guess. Lots of men who have a little
money saved up can get a pull. They lend money,
and then they can make the men to whom they lend
it do about as they like, by threatening to take

their land away from them if they don't pay up
their mortgages as soon as they're due. It's
pretty bad business, but that's the way things are.
I'm afraid we're going to have a lot of trouble,
and until I know just what's what, I've got to do
a lot of my work in the dark. But I'm going to
do my best.''

''I know how Jake Hoover found I was here,
I bet,'' said Bessie, who had been thinking hard.

''How, Bessie?''

''Well, you know General Seeley thought I'd
frightened his pheasants and taken the eggs.
And then, later, I found Jake was the one. General Seeley didn't punish him, but let him go with
a warning.''

''He's too soft-hearted,'' commented Jamieson,
angrily. ''A lad like that ought to be sent to the
reformatory—proper place for him!''

''Well, anyhow,'' Bessie resumed, smiling at
the young lawyer's vehemence, and at the look of
approval that Zara shot at him, since she had
felt just the same way about Jake, ''he was turned

away, and I guess he just hung around to see
what I'd do, and where I'd go. I think he'd like
to get even with me, if he could.''

''He'd better behave himself if he's going to
stay around here,'' said Jamieson. ''His mother
won't be around to make people believe that he
hasn't done anything wrong, and he won't find
everyone as lenient and forgiving as General
Seeley when he's caught in the act of doing something he can be sent to jail for. Not if I've got
anything to say about it, he won't!''

''I don't believe he'll be able to stay around
here very long,'' said Bessie, pacifically. ''It
must cost him a lot of money to stay here in the
city, and I don't know how he can manage that.
Maw Hoover always gave him money whenever
he wanted it, if she had it, but she never had very
much.''

''That's good,'' said the lawyer. ''We'll hope
that he'll be starved out pretty soon, and have
to go home. But I guess we'd better not count
very much on that. He may find someone who's

anxious enough to make trouble for you two to pay him to stay here for a while. He'd be pretty useful, I imagine.''

''I think we're foolish to do so much guessing,'' said Eleanor, suddenly. ''You can know much better what to do when you've really found something out, Charlie. Now, listen. I was thinking of letting these two go to work for a little while before we went to the farm, so that they could earn some money for themselves.''

''Yes,'' said Bessie and Zara, in one breath, eagerly. ''We're so anxious to do that. We mustn't keep on living here and taking charity—''

But the lawyer shook his head vigorously.

''Not right away,'' he said. ''It's just because I'm doing so much guessing that we mustn't take any chances, Eleanor. You want to keep them close to you for a while. I spoke about that before Bessie saw our young friend Hoover, and I think so more than ever now. Don't you see that they're being spied on already?''

''I certainly do,'' said Eleanor. ''And I just

want to do whatever is best for them. Bessie, you mustn't think you're getting charity when you stay here. You're here as my guests, and we love to have you—both of you."

"That's right, Bessie," said Jamieson, smiling. "She means that, or she wouldn't say it. I can tell you you were mighty lucky when you ran into Eleanor the way you did."

"We know that, Mr. Jamieson; we do, indeed!"

"Nonsense!" said Eleanor, flushing, but not really displeased by the compliment, which was evidently sincere. "I believe anyone would have done just what I did."

"I wish I had your faith in human nature, Eleanor, but I haven't and I know that mighty few people would have been willing to do it, even if they'd been able. You've got to remember that, too. Lots of people couldn't have done what you did. Well, I've got to be going."

"You'll call for us tomorrow, though, won't you, Charlie, to take Zara to see her father?"

"Yes, indeed. I won't fail you. He's looking

2—C3

forward to it, and I've got an idea, or I hope, at least, that when he finds I've kept my promise and brought Zara to see him, he'll feel more like trusting me.''

"I'm sure he will when I tell him how good you've been to us, Mr. Jamieson,'' said Zara.

"Better not tell him about my goodness until I've done something beside talk, Zara. But I'm going to do my best anyhow, and I'm sure things will come out right in the end. Just keep smiling, be cheerful, and don't worry any more than you can help.''

From the porch they watched him walk off down the street. He carried himself like the athlete he was, and his broad shoulders and fine, free stride were those of a man who inspires confidence and trust, even in those who only see his back.

"Look!'' said Zara, suddenly. "Why is Jake Hoover going down that way? And isn't he acting queerly?''

"Why, I believe he's following Mr. Jamieson!'' said Bessie. "See, he keeps getting behind trees and things, and he's staying on the other side of the street. Whenever Mr. Jamieson turns, Jake hides himself.''

Eleanor frowned thoughtfully.

"I think you're right, Bessie,'' she said. "And I know what I'm going to do. I'm going to telephone to his office and tell his clerk to slip out and meet him, so that he can warn him. He ought to know about that.''

She went in hurriedly to use the telephone.

"I'm going upstairs to get my handkerchief,'' said Zara. "My, isn't it warm?''

So Bessie was left alone on the piazza. She was afraid of Jake Hoover; afraid of the mischief he might do, that is. No longer was she afraid of him as she had been in the old days on the farm, when he had bullied her and made her the scapegoat for all the offences he could possibly load on her slim shoulders. One night in the woods, when Bessie, wrapped in a sheet and playing ghost, had frightened Jake and his mischievous friends away before they could terrify the Camp

Fire Girls as they lay asleep, had taught Bessie that Jake was a coward.

"It's Zara they're after—not me," Bessie thought to herself. "I've been out alone ever and ever so often, and there's no one here to hurt me. I'm going to go after Jake myself, and try to see what he's up to."

At first Bessie's pursuit led her along the pleasant, tree-shaded streets of the suburb where the Mercers lived. Bessie had never been in the city before and all was strange to her. But here it seemed to her that the stories she had read of crowded streets must have been exaggerated, for she saw few people. Sometimes automobiles passed her, and delivery wagons, and a few children were playing here and there. But there were no high buildings, and it seemed almost as peaceful as it had around Hedgeville.

But then gradually, as she went on, conditions changed. She crossed a street on which there ran a street car line, and there many people were passing. Still she managed to keep Jake Hoover

in sight, and, though she could not always see
Charlie Jamieson, she supposed that Jake could,
and it was Jake she was following, after all.

More than once Jake turned and looked behind
him, and Bessie had to be constantly on her guard
lest he discover her. At first it was easy enough
to escape his eye—she had only to dodge behind a
tree. But as she drew nearer and nearer to the
business part of the town the trees began to dis-
appear. There was no more green grass between
the pavement and the street itself; the pavements
were narrower, and they were needed for the
crowds that passed quickly along. But in those
very crowds Bessie found a substitute for the
trees. She felt that they would protect her and
cover her movements, and she increased her pace,
so that she could get nearer to Jake, and so run
less risk of losing him in the crowd.

No one paid any attention to her, and that
seemed strange to Bessie, used to the curiosity of
country folk regarding any stranger, although
Zara, who knew more about city life, had told

her that it would be so. She was grateful, anyhow; she wanted to be let alone. And evidently
Jake was profiting by the same indifference.

Her chase led her before long into the most
thickly settled part of the city. Trolley cars
clanged past her all the time now; the center of
the street was full of vehicles of all sorts, and, as
she hurried along, she was hard put to it to keep
her feet, so great was the rush and the hurry of
those with whom she shared the pavement.

Then she came to a sort of central square, where
all the business of the town seemed to be concen-
trated. On one side was a great building. Outside were cabs and newsboys, and Bessie recognized it as the station through which, with Eleanor
Mercer and the rest of the Camp Fire Girls, she
had come to the city. Bessie stopped at the curb,
dazed and confused. Here she lost sight of Jake.

After her long chase, that seemed bitterly hard.
Had she only known what was coming, she would
have been closer to him, but, as it was, she could
only stand on the corner, looking helplessly about,

on the off chance that she would again catch sight
of his well-known figure.

But luck was not with her. Even someone far
better used to the bustle and confusion of the city
might well have been at a loss. It was the luncheon hour, and from all the buildings hundreds of
people were pouring out, making the streets seem
fuller than ever. And it was not long before
Bessie decided with a sigh that she must give up,
and find her way home. She was afraid Eleanor
Mercer would be worried and alarmed by her
absence, and she determined to return as she had
come, and as fast as she could.

Still, on the way, surely she could peep into
one of the beautiful store windows—and she did.
For a moment she stood there, and then, suddenly, she felt a hand in her pocket. She turned
to see whose it was—and looked up into the evil
eyes of Farmer Weeks!

"Stop her!" he cried. "She picked my
pocket!"

CHAPTER III

Bessie gasped in sheer terror, and for a moment she couldn't open her mouth. Farmer Weeks, his weather-beaten face twisted into a grin of malice and dislike, stood looking down at her, his bony hand gripping her wrist. Even had it been in Bessie's mind to run away, she could not have done it. And, as a matter of fact, the shock of hearing his voice, of seeing him, and, above all, of being accused of such a thing, had deprived her for the moment of the use of her legs as well as of the power of speech.

Then, while Farmer Weeks lifted his voice again, calling for a policeman, Bessie got a vivid and sharp lesson in the interest a city crowd can be induced to take in anything out of the ordinary, no matter how trifling. The pavement where they stood was densely crowded already. Now more people seemed to spring up from nowhere at all, and they were surrounded by a ring of people who pressed against one another, calling curious questions, all trying to get into the front rank to see whatever was to be seen.

"Gosh all hemlock!" Farmer Weeks confided to the crowd. "They told me to look out fer them scalawags when I come to taown, but I swan I didn't expect to see a gal like that tryin' to lift my wallet. No, sir! But they got to get up pretty early in the mornin' to fool me—they have that!"

Even in her fright, Bessie divined at once what the old rascal was trying to do. He was playing the part of the green and unsuspicious country-man, the farmer on a trip, usually the easy prey of sharpers of all sorts, and he was doing it for a purpose—to win the sympathy of the crowd. In her new clothes Bessie looked enough like a city girl to pass for one easily, while Farmer Weeks wore old-fashioned clothes of rusty black, a slouch hat, and a colored handkerchief knotted about his neck in place of a scarf. He carried an

old-fashioned cotton umbrella, too, a huge affair
—a regular "bumbleshoot," and he was dressed
to play the part.

"Hey, mister, gimme a nickel an' I'll call a cop
for you!" volunteered a small, sharp-faced boy,
with a bundle of papers under his arm. Somehow
he had managed to squirm through the crowd.

Weeks looked at him reproachfully.

"You call a constable—an' I'll give you the
nickel when you come back with him," he said.

In spite of her deplorable situation, Bessie
wanted to laugh. It was so like Farmer Weeks,
the miser, to be unwilling to risk even five cents
without being sure that he would get value for
his money! The boy darted off, and Bessie heard
half a dozen of the crowd make remarks applaud-
ing the good sense of her supposed victim.

"Ain't it too bad?" said Weeks tolerantly to
the crowd, as he waited for a policeman, still
clutching Bessie's hand tightly. "Who'd ever
think a pretty young gal like her would try to
rob an old man—hey?"

"Never can tell, Pop," said a keen-eyed youth, who was standing near. His eyes darted nervously about from one face to another. "Them as you wouldn't suspect naturally is the worst, as a rule —it's so easy for them to make a get-away."

Then the crowd gave way suddenly for a man in a blue uniform, but Bessie, still unable to say anything, saw at once it was not a policeman. But it was not until he was quite close to her that she recognized him with a little thrill of joy. And at the same moment he recognized her, too, as well as Farmer Weeks. It was Tom Norris, the friendly train conductor who had helped Zara and herself to escape to Pine Bridge, and out of the state in which Hedgeville was situated.

"Come, come; what's this?" asked the train conductor sharply. "Let go of that girl's arm, you Weeks!"

"What business is it of your'n?" asked Weeks, angrily.

"You let her go," said Norris, with determination, "or I'll pretty soon show you what business

it is of mine—I'll knock you down, white hair and
all! You ought to be ashamed of yourself, pickin'
on the girl this way!"

He advanced, threateningly, and none of the
crowd undertook to protect Weeks from his ob-
vious anger. Norris was a big, strong man, and,
for all his kindly ways, it was evident that he
could fight well if he saw any reason for doing
it. And now, it was plain, he thought the reason
was excellent, and he was entirely ready to back
up what he had to say with his sturdy fists. Weeks
saw that plainly, and he had reason to fear the
burly conductor. Quickly he released Bessie's
wrist, and a moment later Norris would have had
her out of the crush had not the arrival of another man in uniform created a diversion. This
time it really was a policeman, and he came at
the heels of the newsboy who had run after him.

"Here's yer cop, mister! Now gimme the
nickel!" said the boy shrilly to the farmer.

"Run along! I never promised you no nickel,"
said Farmer Weeks, looking nervously at Norris.

But at that the crowd, which had been disposed to side with him, transferred its sympathies suddenly to the cheated newsboy, who was pouring out a stream of angry words, the while he clung to Weeks' arm, demanding his money.

Weeks soon saw that he had better not try to save a nickel, much as he valued it, and, reluctantly enough, he drew a purse from his trousers pocket and gave the boy his money, counting out five pennies.

"Here, here; what's all this fuss about?" asked the policeman. He was responsible for keeping order on his post, and before Weeks could answer his question he drove the crowd away with sharp orders to move on and be quick about it. Then he turned back to the farmer, Bessie, and the conductor, who had taken Bessie's hand.

"Now then, whose pocket was picked? Yours, young lady?"

"No, consarn ye, mine!" said Farmer Weeks, angrily, as he heard the question. "And she done it, too—she's a slick one, she is! An' this fresh

railroad man here was tryin' to help her get away.
Like as not they work together, an' he was fixin'
to have her give him half of what she got.''

Norris smiled at the policeman.

"You know me, Mike," he said. "Think I'm
in that sort of business?"

"Begorra, an' I know ye're not!" said the
policeman, indignantly. "Talk straight, now, you
old rube, an' tell me what it is you're tryin' to
say. What sort of a charge ye're after makin'?"

"She put her hand in my pocket—an' she stole
my wallet," said Farmer Weeks. "She's got it
in her pocket now—her right-hand pocket!"

"How do you know that?" asked the policeman,
sharply.

"How—why shouldn't I know? Look and see
for yourself—"

But there was no need. Bessie herself, tears
in her eyes, plunged her hand into the pocket
Weeks had named—and, to her consternation,
the wallet came out in her hand. She stared at
it in stupefaction.

"I don't know how it got there! I never saw
it before!" she exclaimed.

"H'm! This looks pretty bad, Tom," said the
policeman. "Is this young lady a friend of
yours?"

"She is that," said Tom, stoutly. "And I'll
go bail for her anywhere. She never picked that
old scalawag's pocket. I know him well, Mike,
and I've never known any good of him. He never
rides on my train without tryin' to beat the company out of the fare—uses every old trick you
ever heard of. Many's the time I've had to
threaten to put him off between stations before
he'd fork over the money."

But Mike, the policeman, looked doubtful, as
well he might, and there was a gleam of evil
triumph in the farmer's eyes.

"Listen here!" said Tom, suddenly. "He says
that's his wallet, and he's makin' enough fuss for
it to have a thousand dollars inside. But when
he paid the boy he took a purse from his pocket
to get the money."

"That's right. I seen him myself," said Mike, still scratching his head. "I'll just have a look inside that pocket-book."

"Ye will not—that's my property!" said Farmer Weeks, reaching quickly for the wallet.

But Mike was too quick for him, and in a moment he had opened the wallet, and could see that it was empty, except for a few torn pieces of paper, evidently put in it to stuff it out, and deceive people into thinking that it contained a wad of bills.

"What sort of game are yez tryin' to put up on us here?" demanded the policeman, angrily. "Here, take yer book—"

"She's as much guilty of theft as if there had been a hundred dollars in it," said Farmer Weeks, recovering from his dismay at the exposure of the trick. "You arrest her or I'll—"

"What will yez do, ye spalpeen?" said the policeman. "If ye get gay wid me I'll run yez in—and don't be after forgettin' that, either!"

As he spoke he turned, angrily, to observe a small boy who was tugging at his sleeve.

"Say, mister, say," begged the boy, "listen here a minute, will yer? I seen the old guy slip his purse into her pocket. She never took it."

Tom's eyes, as he heard, lighted up.

"By Gad, Mike, that's what he did!" he exclaimed. "Did you hear how ready he was to tell just which pocket she had it in? How'd he have known that—unless he put it there, eh?"

"It's a lie!" stormed Farmer Weeks. "Here, are you going to lock that girl up as a thief or not?"

"Indade and I'm not," said the officer, warmly. "Drop her wrist—quick!"

He stepped forward as he spoke, and Weeks, seeing by the gleam in the Irishman's eye that he had gone too far, quickly released Bessie. As she moved away from him he stood still, red-eyed and trembling with rage.

"An' what's more, you old scalawag," said the policeman, "I'm going to run *you* in. May-

be you never heard tell of perjury, but it's
worse than picki ' pockets, let me tell you.''

His heavy hand dropped to Weeks' shoulder,
but he was too slow. With a yell of fright the
old farmer, displaying an agility with which no
one would have been ready to credit him, turned
and dove headlong through the crowd.

The policeman started to give chase, but Tom
Norris restrained him. He was laughing heartily.

''What's the use? Let him be, Mike,'' he said.
''My, but it was as good as a play to see you
handle him. Gosh! Watch the old beggar run,
will you?''

Indeed, Weeks was running as fast as he could,
and, even as they watched him, he disappeared
inside the station.

''That's a good riddance. Maybe he'll go
home and stay there,'' said the conductor. ''He
won't try his dirty tricks on you again,'' he
added, turning to Bessie. ''If he does, you'll
have a friend in Mike, here.''

"True for you, Tom Norris!" said the policeman. "I'm glad ye turned up boy. Ye saved
me from makin' a fool of meself, I'm thinkin'.
The old omadhoun! To think he'd put up a job
like that on a slip of a girl, and him ould enough
to be her father—or her grandfather!"

"Well, I've helped you out again, haven't
I?" said Tom Norris. "Are you living here in
the city now? Suppose you tell me why old
Weeks is so mean to you, now that we've the
time."

"I will, and gladly," said Bessie. "But I
haven't so very much time. Can you walk with
me as I go home?"

So, with Tom Norris to look after her, Bessie
began her trip back to the Mercer house, and,
on the way, she told him the story of her flight
from Hedgeville, and the adventures that had
happened since its beginning.

"I suppose I was foolish to go after Jake
Hoover that way," she concluded, "but I thought
I might be able to help. I didn't like to see

him following Mr. Jamieson that way, when he was trying to be so nice to us.''

"Maybe you were foolish,'' said Tom. "But don't let it worry you too much. You meant well, and I guess there's lots of us are foolish without having as good an excuse as that.''

"Oh, there's Mr. Jamieson now!'' cried Bessie, suddenly spying the young lawyer on the other side of the street. "I think I'd better tell him what's happened, don't you, Mr. Norris?''

"I do indeed. Stay here, I'll run over. The young fellow with the brown suit, is it?''

Bessie nodded, and Tom Norris ran across the street and was back in a moment with Jamieson, who was mightily surprised to see Bessie, whom he had left only a short time before at the Mercer house. He frowned very thoughtfully as he heard her story.

"I'm not going to scold you for taking such a risk,'' he said. "I really didn't think, either, that it was you they would try to harm. I thought your friend Zara was the only one who was in danger.''

"I suppose they'd try to get hold of Miss Bessie here, though,'' said the conductor, "because they'd think she'd be a good witness, perhaps, if there was any business in court. I don't know much about the law, except I think it's a good thing to keep clear of.''

"You bet it is,'' said Jamieson, with a laugh.

"That's fine talk, from a lawyer!'' smiled Tom Norris. "Ain't it your business to get people into lawsuits?''

"Not a bit of it!'' said Jamieson. "A good lawyer keeps his clients out of court. He saves money for them that way, and they run less risk of being beaten. The biggest cases I have never get into court at all. It's only the shyster lawyers, like Isaac Brack, who are always going to court, whether there's any real reason for it or not.''

"Brack?'' said Tom. "Why, say, I know him! And, what's more, this man Weeks does, too.

Brack's his lawyer. I heard that a long time ago. Brack gets about half the cases against the railroad, too. Whenever there's a little accident, Brack hunts up the people who might have been hurt, and tries to get damages for them. Only, if he wins a case for them, he keeps most of the money—and if they lose he charges them enough so that he comes out ahead, anyhow.''

"That's the fellow," Jamieson said. "We'll get him disbarred sooner or later, too. He's a bad egg. I'm glad to know I've got to fight him in this case. If this young Hoover was following me, I'll bet Brack had something to do with it.''

"He was certainly following you," said Bessie. "Whenever you turned around he got behind a tree or something, so that you wouldn't see him.''

"He needn't have been so careful. He might have walked right next to me all the way into town, and I'd never have suspected him. As it happened, I wasn't going anywhere this morning —anywhere in particular, I mean. It wouldn't have made any difference if Brack had known just what I was doing. But I'm mighty glad to know that he is trying to spy on me, Bessie. In the next few days I'm apt to do some things I wouldn't want him to know about at all, and now that I'm warned I'll be able to keep my eyes and my ears open, and I guess Brack and his spies will have some trouble in getting on to anything I choose to keep hidden from them."

"That's the stuff!" approved Tom. "I told Miss Bessie here she'd done all right. She meant well, even if she did run a foolish risk. And there's no harm done."

"Well, we'd better hurry home," said Jamieson. "I don't want them to be worried about you, Bessie, so I'll take you home in a taxicab."

The cab took them swiftly toward the Mercer house. When they were still two or three blocks away Jamieson started and pointed out a man on the sidewalk to Bessie.

"There's Brack now!" he exclaimed. "See, Bessie? That little man, with the eyeglasses.

He's up to some mischief. I wonder what he's doing out this way?"

When they arrived, Eleanor Mercer, her eyes showing that she was worried, was waiting for them on the porch.

"Oh, I'm so glad you're here!" she exclaimed.

"I'm so sorry if you were worried about me, Miss Eleanor," said Bessie, remorsefully.

"I wasn't, though," said Eleanor. "It's Zara! She's upstairs, crying her eyes out and she won't answer me when I try to get her to tell me what's wrong. You'd better see her, Bessie."

CHAPTER IV

Alarmed at this news of Zara, Bessie hurried upstairs at once to the room the two girls shared. She found her chum on the bed, crying as if her heart would break.

"Why, Zara, what's the matter? Why are you crying?" she asked.

But try as she might, Bessie could get no answer at all from Zara for a long time.

"Have I done anything to make you feel bad? Has anything gone wrong here?" urged Bessie. "If you'll only tell us what's the matter, dear, we'll straighten it out. Can't you trust me?"

"N—nothing's happened—you haven't done anything," Zara managed to say at last.

"Surely nothing Miss Eleanor has said has hurt you, Zara? I'm certain she'd feel terrible

59

if she thought you were crying because of anything she had done!"

Zara shook her head vehemently at that, but her sobs only seemed to come harder than before.

Bessie was thoroughly puzzled. She knew that Zara, brought up in a foreign country, did not always understand American ways. Sometimes, when Bessie had first known her, little jesting remarks, which couldn't have been taken amiss by any American girl, had reduced her to tears. And Bessie thought it entirely possible that someone, either Miss Eleanor, or her mother, or one of the Mercer servants, might have offended Zara without in the least meaning to do so.

But Zara seemed determined to keep the cause of her woe to herself. Not all of Bessie's pleading could make her answer the simplest questions. Finally, seeming to feel a little better, she managed to speak more coherently.

"Leave me alone for a little while, please,

Bessie," she begged. "I'll be all right then—really I will!"

So Bessie, reluctantly enough, had to go downstairs, since she understood thoroughly that to keep on pressing Zara for an explanation while she was in such a nervous state would do more harm than good.

"Could you find out what was wrong?" asked Eleanor anxiously when Bessie came down. Charlie Jamieson was still with her on the porch, smoking a cigar and frowning as if he were thinking of something very unpleasant. He was, as a matter of fact. He was changing all his ideas of the case in which Eleanor's encounter with the two girls had involved him, since, with Brack for an opponent, he knew only too well that he was in for a hard fight, and if, as he supposed, the opposition was entirely without a reasonable case, a fight in which dirty and unfair methods were sure to be employed.

Bessie shook her head.

"She wouldn't tell me anything—just begged

me to leave her alone and said she'd be all right presently," she answered. "I've seen her this way before and, really, there's nothing to do but wait until she feels better."

"You've seen her this way before, you say?" said Jamieson, quickly. "What was the matter then? What made her act so? If we know why she did it before, perhaps it will give us a clew to why she is behaving in such a queer fashion now."

Bessie hesitated.

"She's awfully sensitive," she said. "Sometimes, when people have just joked with her a little bit, without meaning to say anything nasty at all, she's thought they were angry at her, or laughing at her for being a foreigner, and she's gone off just like this. I thought at first—"

"Yes?" said Eleanor, encouragingly, when Bessie stopped. "Don't be afraid to tell us what you think, Bessie. We just want to get to the bottom of this strange fit of hers, you know."

"Well, it seems awfully mean to say it,"

said poor Bessie, "when you've been so lovely to us, but I thought maybe someone had joked about her in some way. You know she sometimes pronounces words in a funny fashion, as if she'd only read them, and had never heard anyone speak them. In Hedgeville lots of people used to laugh at her for that. I think that's why she stopped going to school. And I thought, perhaps, that was what was the matter—"

"It might have happened, of course," said Eleanor, "and without anyone meaning to hurt her feelings. I'd be very careful myself, but some of the other people around the house wouldn't know, of course. But, no, that won't explain it, Bessie. Not this time."

"Are you sure, Eleanor?" asked Jamieson.

"Positively," she answered. "Because, after you went off, she was out here with me for quite a long time. Then I was called inside, and I'm quite sure no one from the house saw her at all after that until I found her crying. She'd been outside on the porch all the time—"

"Aha!" cried Jamieson, then. "If no one in the house here talked to her, someone from outside must have done it. Listen, Bessie. She wouldn't go off that way just from brooding, would she, just from thinking about things?"

"No, I'm quite sure she wouldn't, Mr. Jamieson. She's felt bad two or three times since we left Hedgeville, when she got to thinking about her father's troubles, and everything of that sort. But she's always told me about it and it hasn't made her feel just as she seems to now, anyhow."

"Well, then, can't you see? No one here said anything to her, so it must have been someone who isn't in the house—someone who spoke to her after you left her out here alone, Eleanor. And I know who it was, too!"

"That nasty looking man you pointed out to me as we were coming along with Mr. Norris?" cried Bessie.

"Yes, indeed—Brack!" said Jamieson. "He's just the one who would do it, too! Oh, I tell

you, one has to look out for him! He's as mean
as a man could be and still live, I guess. I've
heard of more harsh, miserable things he's done
than I could tell you in a week. Whenever he's
around it's a warning to look out for trouble.
Suppose you go up to her, Bessie, and see if
mentioning his name will loosen her tongue."

But just as she was entering the house Zara,
with only her reddened eyes to show that she had
been crying at all, came out on the porch.

"I'm ever so ashamed of myself, Miss Eleanor," she said, smiling pluckily. "I suppose you
think I'm an awful cry-baby, but I was just feeling bad about my father and everything, and I
couldn't seem to help it."

Bessie looked at Zara in astonishment. To the
eyes of those who didn't know her as well as
Bessie, Zara might seem to be all right, but Bessie could see that her chum was still frightened
and weak. She wondered why Zara was acting,
for acting she was. She meant that Miss Mercer
and everyone should think that her fit of depres-

2—C5

sion had been only temporary, and that **now** everything was all right. And Bessie, **loyal as ever,** decided to help her.

But when Charlie Jamieson took his **leave** again to go back to his office and his interrupted work, he looked at her keenly and when he started to go he took Bessie by the hand playfully and pulled her off the porch, and out of sight of the others.

"Listen," he said, earnestly, "there's something more than we know about or can guess very easily the matter with your friend, Bessie. She's been frightened—badly frightened. And it's dollars to doughnuts that it's that scoundrel Brack who's frightened her, too. Keep your eyes on her—see that she doesn't get a chance to speak to him or anyone else alone."

"Do you think there's any danger of his coming back?" asked Bessie, alarmed by his serious tone.

"I don't know, Bessie, but I do know **Brack.** And I've found out this much about him. **He's** like a rabbit—he'll fight when he's driven into a corner. And the time he's most dangerous is when he seems to be beaten, when it looks as if he hadn't a leg to stand on."

"Do you think he's beaten now, Mr. Jamieson?"

"No, I don't! And just because he's the man he is. If it were anyone else, I'd say yes, because I don't see what they can expect to do. But you can depend upon it that Brack has some dirty trick up his sleeve, and from all you tell me of this man Weeks, he's the same sort of an ugly customer. So you keep your eyes open, and if anything happens to worry you, call me up right away. Get me at my office if it's before five o'clock; after that, call up this number."

He wrote down a telephone number on a slip of paper and handed it to Bessie.

"That's the telephone at my home, and if I'm not there myself ask for my servant, Farrell. He'll be there, and he'll manage to get word to me somehow, no matter where I am."

"Oh, I do hope I shan't have to bother you, Mr. Jamieson."

"Don't you worry about that. That's what I'm here for, to be bothered, as you call it, if there's any need of me. Remember that you can't do everything yourself—and you may only get into trouble yourself without really helping if you try to do it all. So call on me if there's any need. And, whatever you do, don't let Zara go out of the house alone on any pretence. Remember that, will you?"

"I certainly will, Mr. Jamieson. You're awfully good to us, and I know Zara would be grateful, too, if she were herself. She will be as soon as all this trouble is over."

"I know that, Bessie. Don't you fuss around being grateful to me until I've really done something for you. You know, you're the sort of girl I like. You've got pluck, and you don't get discouraged, like so many girls—though Heaven knows you've had enough trouble to make you as nervous as any of them."

"I get awfully frightened. Indeed, I do!"

"Of course you do, but you've got pluck enough to admit it. Remember this: the real hero is the man who does what's right, and what he knows he ought to do, even if he's scared so that he's shaking like a leaf. Any fool can do a thing if it doesn't frighten him to do it, and he doesn't deserve any special credit for that. The real bravery is the sort a man shows when he goes into battle, for instance, and wants to turn around and run as soon as he hears the bullets singing over his head."

"I'm sure I would want to do just that—"

"But you wouldn't! That's the point, you see. And you always think things are going to be all right. That's fine—because about half the time we can control the things that happen to us. If we think everything will come right in the end, we can usually make them work out our way. But if we start in thinking that nothing is going to be right, why, then we're licked before we begin, and there's not much use trying at all.

Now, you didn't say Zara would feel differently *if* things came out right. You said she would *when* everything was straightened out. And that's the spirit that wins. Try to put some more of it into her, and try to make her tell you what happened, too.''

But all of Bessie's efforts to win Zara's confidence that day were in vain. Zara, however, seemed to be all right. She was brighter and livelier than she had been since Bessie had known her. All day long she laughed and burst into little snatches of song, and Miss Mercer was delighted.

Nevertheless Bessie wasn't satisfied, and she kept a close watch on Zara all day. It seemed time wasted, however. Zara made no attempt to keep away from her; seemed anxious, indeed, to be with her chum, that they might talk over their plans for winning enough honors as Camp Fire Girls to become Fire-Makers.

Had Bessie's eyes and her perceptions been less keen she would have thought her first idea, the one she shared with Charlie Jamieson, a mistaken one. But more than once, when Zara thought she was unobserved, and was therefore off her guard, Bessie saw the corners of her mouth droop and a wistful look come into her eyes. There was fear in those eyes, too, though of what, Bessie could not imagine.

It was long after midnight that night when Bessie was aroused, she scarcely knew how. Some instinct led her to turn on the light—and she could scarcely repress a scream when she saw that Zara's bed was empty!

CHAPTER V

For a moment she stood in the middle of the room, dazed, wondering what could have happened. The door was closed. Bessie rushed to it, and looked out, but there was no sign of Zara in the hall. She listened intently. The house was silent, with the silence that broods over a well regulated house at night, when everyone is or ought to be asleep. But then there was a noise from outside—a noise that came through the windows, from the street.

Bessie rushed back into the room and over to the window. She knew now that the noise she heard was the same one that had awakened her.

And, looking out of the window, Bessie saw what had made the noise—a big, green automobile, that, even as she looked, was gliding slowly

73

but with increasing speed away from the Mercer house. She stood rooted to the spot, unable to cry out, or to make a move. But somehow, though she could never explain afterward how it happened, since the importance of it did not strike her at all at the time, Bessie managed to get a mental photograph of one thing that was to prove important in the extreme—the number of the automobile, plainly visible in the light of the tail lamp that shone full upon it. The figures were registered in her brain as if she had studied them for an hour in the effort to memorize them— 4587.

Then, when the car was out of sight around the corner, Bessie's power of movement seemed to be restored to her as mysteriously as it had been taken away. Her first impulse was to cry out and arouse the household. But the futility of that soon struck her, and she remembered what Charlie Jamieson had said. If anything happened, if she was frightened, she was to call on him. And certainly something *had* happened.

Of her alarm there could be no doubt. She was shaking like a leaf, as if she were exposed to a cold wind, although the night was hot and even sultry.

Swiftly she sought for and found the telephone number the lawyer had written down for her. Then, in her bare feet, lest she make a noise and arouse the whole household, she crept downstairs to reach the telephone.

"Oh, I do hope they won't see me or hear me," she breathed to herself. "There's nothing they can do, and maybe, if I get hold of Mr. Jamieson at once, we can have Zara back before they know she's gone."

At that hour of the night it was hard work to get the connection she wanted, and Bessie chafed at the delay, knowing that every moment might be precious, were Zara in real danger. But she got the number at last, after Central had tried to convince her no one would answer at such a time.

"What's happened? Has something gone

wrong?'' Jamieson asked anxiously as soon as he recognized her voice.

"Oh, I'm terribly afraid it has—and it was all my fault! I was asleep, Mr. Jamieson—and Zara's gone!"

"By herself, or don't you know?"

"I don't know positively, but I think she was taken off in a big automobile. But, Mr. Jamieson, I think she wanted to go!"

"Why, what makes you think that?"

"She's taken all the things that were given to her. And then, she got out so quietly that I didn't hear her. If anyone had carried her away, they'd have waked me up, I'm sure."

"That's bad—if she went away of her own accord. Makes it harder to find her, harder to get her back."

"What shall we do, Mr. Jamieson? You will try to get her back, won't you, even if she did go with them willingly?"

"Yes, yes, of course! I'll come out right

away. Better not tell the others yet, if you
haven't done it already."

Then Bessie told him about the automobile,
and the number she had seen.

"Oh, that's different!" he exclaimed. "There's
no use my coming to the house then—not right
away, at least. I'll find out whose car that is
right away—and then perhaps we'll be able to
get a clue more quickly. Someone is almost sure
to have noticed that number, you see. Policemen
have a way of keeping their eyes on car numbers
as late as this, just on the chance that there may
be something wrong about people who are chasing around in this town when they ought to be
in bed. You go back to sleep, if you can. I'll
let you know as soon as there's something new."

"I don't see how I can sleep, Mr. Jamieson.
Isn't there something I can do, please? That
would make me feel ever so much better, I'm
sure."

"I know, I know! But there isn't a thing you
can do to-night. There's precious little I can

do, for that matter, myself. You get some rest, so that you'll be fresh and strong in the morning. No telling what may turn up then; and we may need you to do a whole lot. Got to keep yourself in condition, you know. Remember that, always. That's the way to help. Good-night! I'm going to hurry out now and see what I can find out about that car.''

So Bessie went back to her room, and, knowing that the lawyer had given her good advice when he had urged her to rest, she tried hard to go to sleep again. But trying to sleep and actually doing it are very different, and Bessie tossed restlessly for the remainder of the night. The sun, shining through her window in the early morning, was the most welcome of all possible sights, and she got up and dressed, glad that the night of inactivity was over, and that the time for action, if action there was to be, was at hand.

Eleanor was shocked and frightened when she heard what had happened.

"I'm sorry you didn't wake me, Bessie," she said. "It must have been dreadful for you, waiting for morning all alone up there. We could have talked, anyhow, and sometimes that helps a good deal."

"Well, I didn't see any use in spoiling the night for you and I'd have stayed awake anyhow, I think, even if I hadn't been alone. So there was no use keeping you up and awake, too."

"I'll telephone at once and see if anything has been found out, Bessie. Then we'll know better what to do. But I'm afraid there's not much that we can do—not just now."

Jamieson was not in his office, or at his home, when Eleanor telephoned. But when she stopped to think she realized that he was almost certain to be busy in his search for some clue to the missing girl.

"Come with me. Let's go down town," she said to Bessie. "I want to get some things for you, anyhow, and anything is better than sitting around the house here, just waiting for news. That's terrible. Don't you think so?"

"Yes, indeed. But suppose some news came when we were out?"

"Oh, we can easily telephone to the house and then, if there should be a message, we can get it right away, you see. I'll tell them here to write down any message that comes, and we'll telephone every fifteen minutes or so."

"Shall we see Mr. Jamieson while we're down town?"

"Yes, we will. That's a good idea. It will save his time, too, and there may be something he wants us to do."

So they started. Eleanor wanted to walk. But before they had gone very far a big automobile drew up along the sidewalk, and a cheery, pleasant man, middle aged, with a smiling face, and white hair, though he seemed too young for that, hailed them.

"Hello, Miss Mercer!" he said. "Jump in, won't you? I'll take you wherever you want to go. I've got lots of time—nothing in the world to do, and I'm lonely.''

"Why, thank you very much, Mr. Holmes,'' said Eleanor, smiling at him. "This is my new friend, Bessie King, Mr. Holmes. Mr. Holmes is one of our family's oldest and best friends.''

"Well, well, this is very nice!" he said. "I'd better be careful, though, or I'll have all the young fellows in town down on me, when they see an old codger like me driving two pretty young ladies around. Where shall we go, eh?''

"If you're really not in a hurry, Mr. Holmes,'' said Eleanor, "I wish you would take us down town by the long way around. I'd like Bessie to see the river and the Kent Bridge.''

"Splendid!" said Mr. Holmes. "That's fine! You see, they say I'm a back number, now that I don't know how to run my store any more. I guess they're right, too. I just seem to be in the way when I go down there. So I stay away as long as I can find anything else to do.''

2—C6

Eleanor laughed, but Bessie somehow felt that the jovial words didn't ring true. There was a strange look in the eyes of their kindly host, and despite her attempts to convince herself that she was foolish, she didn't like him. But she enjoyed the ride thoroughly. He took them out of the town, and then, skirting the suburbs by a beautiful road, approached the heart of the business section by a new road that Bessie had not seen before. But then, though he had said, and, indeed, proved, that he was in no hurry, Mr. Holmes began to increase the speed of his car.

"He's going very fast if he's not in a hurry," suggested Bessie, sure that the driver could not hear in the rush of the wind made by the car's speed.

Eleanor laughed merrily.

"He always does everything in a hurry," she said. "This is the fastest car in town, and before automobiles got so popular, Mr. Holmes had the fastest horses. He just likes to go quickly. That's why his business was so successful, they say.''

Just then the car stopped, and Holmes, laughing, turned to them.

"I heard that,'' he said. "After all, what's the harm? It would have taken you an hour to get down town if you'd walked all the way, wouldn't it, Miss Eleanor?''

She nodded.

"All right, then, I'll get you there as soon as that, and have time for a bit of a spin in the country, as well. We'll go pretty fast, so just put on these goggles, young ladies, and you'll have no trouble getting specks in your eyes. I'll do the same. I really intended to drive slowly today—that's why I haven't got mine on. But somehow, when I get a wheel between my hands, I can't drive slowly; it isn't in me, somehow!''

He handed them their goggles, and then put on his own, and changed his soft hat, which had two or three times threatened to blow off, for a cap that would stay on in any wind. And, as he faced them, Bessie had all she could do to suppress a sharp cry of amazement, and she was more than thankful for the goggles that partly concealed her start of surprise and dismay. For the sight of Holmes, thus equipped, had recalled something that seemed in a way, at least, to explain her feeling of distrust and dislike.

Eleanor saw that Bessie was troubled, even though Holmes was ignorant of the sensation he had caused, and, as soon as the car was moving at high speed again, she leaned over close.

"What is it, Bessie? What startled you so?"

"I'll tell you later, Miss Eleanor," whispered Bessie. "I'm not sure enough yet—really I'm not! But as soon as I am, I'll tell you all I know."

Mr. Holmes was as good as his word. He brought them into the central part of the town just at the time he had promised, and sprang out to open the door of the tonneau for them.

"Must you really go now?" he said, dejectedly. "You'll be leaving me all alone, you know. Can't you finish your shopping, and then let me run you out to Arkville for luncheon?"

"You speak as if it were just across the street," laughed Eleanor. "And you know, Bessie, it's really fifty miles or more away, and it's actually over the state line. It's in your old state—the same one Hedgeville is in. But it's in a different direction, and it's even further from Hedgeville than we are here, I guess. Isn't it, Mr. Holmes?"

"I'd have to know just where Hedgeville is to answer that, Miss Mercer. And I've never been there nor even traveled through it, so far as I can remember. I'll look it up on my road map, though, if you like—"

"Oh, no, please don't bother to do that. It's not of the slightest importance."

"Then we shall have to put off Arkville to another day, you think, Miss Mercer?"

"I'm afraid so, really. We've a good deal to do today, and there are reasons that I won't

bother you with for our having to be in town.
Thank you ever so much for the ride.''

"Yes, thank you ever so much," echoed Bessie.

They were near Charlie Jamieson's office, and,
as the car turned and disappeared in the mass
of traffic, Bessie clutched Eleanor's arm.

"Oh, do come quickly, Miss Eleanor, please!
Look at this. Don't you think we ought to tell
Mr. Jamieson about it right away?"

She held out a piece of ribbon, torn and stained.
It was not large, but there was enough of it to
identify it easily. And, as Eleanor looked at it,
she remembered faintly having seen it before.

"What is that? Where did you find it?" she
asked, puzzled.

"It's the ribbon Zara wore in her hair, and
I found it in the car. It fell on the floor when
he opened the door for us to get out—it must
have been caught there. And do you remember,
we got in on the other side, so that that door
wasn't opened then?"

Eleanor looked more puzzled than ever.

"I don't see how that can be Zara's ribbon," she protested. "What would she have been doing in Mr. Holmes' car? It's just an accident, Bessie. It's just a coincidence that that ribbon should be there. It might have belonged to someone else—I'm sure it did, in fact."

"Oh, please, please, I know!" said Bessie. "Won't you let me tell Mr. Jamieson about it?"

"Oh, yes, of course, but he'll say just what I do, Bessie. You mustn't let this affect you so that you get nervous and hysterical, Bessie. That's not the way to help Zara."

They were walking toward the building in which Jamieson's offices were located, and Bessie was hurrying their progress as much as she could.

"I don't like Mr. Holmes. I'm afraid of him," she said. "I know that sounds dreadful, but it's true—"

"Why, Bessie, how absurd!" she exclaimed. "I've known him for years and years, and he's one of the nicest, kindest men in town."

"But, Miss Eleanor, do you remember when you asked him about Hedgeville, he said he'd never been there?"

"Yes, and I thought, as soon as I asked him, that he would probably have to tell me just that. Hedgeville's out of the way. You never saw automobile parties on trips going through, did you?"

"No, we didn't. About the only people who came there in automobiles came to see someone— and usually Farmer Weeks."

"There, you see!"

"But, Miss Eleanor, Mr. Holmes knows all about Hedgeville! He's been there ever so many times! I thought this morning, as soon as he stopped to talk to you, that I'd seen him before somewhere, but I wasn't sure."

"Why, what do you mean? Are you sure now?"

"Yes, I was sure the minute he put on those goggles and his cap. He's driven to Hedgeville a lot in the last year. The last time wasn't more than three weeks ago, and he was in that same car, and wore the same cap and goggles.''

Eleanor stopped, looking very thoughtful.

''I think you must be mistaken, Bessie,'' she said. ''There's no reason why he shouldn't tell us if he'd ever been there, and he certainly couldn't have forgotten it if he's been there as often as you say. Can't you see that? What object could he have in trying to deceive us?''

''I don't know. I can't guess that unless— well, I can tell you who it was he saw when he was there—every time. It was Farmer Weeks. And I think he was there the day before they took Zara's father away. I'm not sure, but I think so.''

''If you could be certain,'' said Eleanor, doubtfully, ''that would make it different, Bessie. We'll tell Mr. Jamieson, and see what he thinks. But I'm sure you must be mistaken.''

CHAPTER VI

A SUDDEN TURN

Jamieson was in his office when they entered.

"Well, I wondered where you two were!" he exclaimed, by way of greeting. "I tried to get you on the telephone a couple of times, but I supposed you were probably on your way here."

"We telephoned before we left the house, but we understood that you would be busy," said Eleanor. "So we started to walk into town, and Mr. Holmes saw us, and took us for a ride in his car. I hope it hasn't made any difference—that you didn't want us? Have you found out anything, Charlie?"

"No, it didn't make any difference," said the lawyer, gloomily. "As for finding out things, well, I have, and I haven't! There's no trace of Zara, but there's other news."

"What is it?"

"Well, it's mighty queer, I'll say that for it. When I went to see Zara's father this morning, he refused to see me—sent out word that he didn't want me to act as his lawyer any more. He's got another lawyer, and who do you suppose it is?"

The two girls stared at him, surprised and puzzled.

"Brack!" exclaimed Jamieson. "What do you know about that for a mess, eh? If half of what I believe is right, Brack's his worst enemy. He's hand in glove with the people who are responsible for all his trouble, and yet here he goes and gets the scoundrel to act as his lawyer!"

"Oh, what a shame!" said Eleanor, indignantly. "And he wouldn't even see you to explain?"

"Absolutely not! I tried to get them to let me in, and I sent him an urgent message, telling him it was of the utmost importance for us to have a talk, but I couldn't budge him."

Eleanor was flushed with resentment.

"Well, that settles it!" she said, indignantly. "If people don't want to be helped, one can't help them. He and Zara will just have to look out for themselves, I guess. Bessie, don't you think Zara must have gone with those people in the car willingly?"

"Yes, I do," said Bessie. "But—"

"Then I think she and her father are an ungrateful pair, and they deserve anything that happens to them! I'm certainly not going to worry myself about them any more, and I should think you would drop the whole thing, Charlie Jamieson, and attend to your own affairs!"

"Hold on! You're going a bit too fast, Eleanor," he said, laughing lightly. "Let's see what Bessie thinks about it."

Bessie, who had flushed too, but not with anger, when Eleanor thus gave her resentment full play, was glad of the chance to speak.

"I do think Zara went off willingly and of her own accord," she said. "I'm sure of that, because she couldn't have been taken away without my hearing something."

"Well, then," began Eleanor, "doesn't that prove—"

"But if Zara was willing to go off that way, I believe it's because she thought she was doing the right thing," Bessie went on, determinedly. "Someone must have seen her and told her something she believed, though perhaps it wasn't true."

"Of course!" said Jamieson, heartily. "That's what I've thought from the start, and don't you see who it probably was? Why, Brack! He was in the neighborhood yesterday morning and he must have seen her. He might have told her anything—any wild story. You see, we are pretty much in the dark about this affair yet. We don't know why these people are so keen after Zara's father, or why they've put up this job on him. So I don't think I'll get mad and drop it just because Zara and her father have probably been fooled into acting in a way that would seem likely to irritate me."

Eleanor was regretful at once.

"Oh, you're ever so much more sensible than I am, Charlie," she said. "It made me angry to think they were acting so when all we wanted was to help them, and I lost my temper."

"I suspect that that is just what Brack hoped I would do, Eleanor. And it makes me all the more determined to stick to the case. You see, I'm actually lawyer for Zara's father still, and unless I consent to a change of lawyers, he'll have trouble putting Brack in my place. Brack knows that, too, if he doesn't—and he knows, also, that I know one or two things about him that make it a good idea for him to be careful, unless he wants to be disbarred."

"Then you'll keep on working and you'll try to find out what's become of Zara, too?"

"Yes. I looked up the number that Bessie saw—the number of that car. And it's just as I thought. They were careful enough to use a false number. There's no such number recorded as the one that was on the car."

"But don't you suppose you can find anyone who saw it before they had a chance to change the numbers?"

"I'm working on that line now, but we haven't got any reports yet. I've gone to see the district attorney—the one who looks after the counterfeiting cases as well as the other, who's just in charge of local affairs. And I've convinced them that there's something very queer afoot here. Judge Bailey, who will prosecute Zara's father for counterfeiting, agrees with me that it looks as if a case had been worked up against him by someone who wants to make trouble for him, and he's pretty mad at the idea that anyone would dare to use him in such a crooked game. So we'll have a friend there, if I can get any evidence to back our suspicions."

Suddenly Eleanor remembered what Bessie had thought of Mr. Holmes, her suspicion that she had seen him in Hedgeville, and the incident of finding Zara's ribbon. And she made Bessie tell the lawyer her story.

He laughed when he heard it, much to Bessie's distress.

"I don't think very much of that idea," he said. "Mr. Holmes is one of our wealthiest and most respected citizens. He'd never let himself or his car be mixed up in such a business. And I'm sure he doesn't know Brack, and has never had anything to do with him."

"But it is Zara's ribbon! I'm positive of that," insisted Bessie. "And he's the same man I saw at Farmer Weeks' place in Hedgeville, too."

"No, no; I'm afraid you're mistaken, Bessie."

"But the ribbon—why should that be in his car?"

"Let me see it."

She handed him the ribbon, and he looked at it carefully.

"Why, that doesn't seem to be very promising evidence, Bessie," he said. "I suppose you could find ribbon like that in any dry goods store almost anywhere. Thousands of girls must have

2—C7

pieces just like it. Even if it is just the same as
the one Zara wore, that doesn't prove anything.
You'd have to have more evidence than that.
However, I'll keep it in mind. You never can
tell what's going to turn up, and I suppose it's
easily possible to imagine stranger things than
Mr. Holmes being mixed up in this affair. Well,
you can depend upon it that everything possible
is being done, and no one could do more than that.
I wish I knew more, that's all.''

So did Bessie, and she was thinking hard as
they left his office and made their way toward
some of the shops in which, the day before, she
had so longed to be. Feminine instinct has more
than once proved itself superior to masculine
logic, and although both Jamieson and Eleanor
seemed inclined to laugh at her, Bessie felt that
she was right—that Mr. Holmes, in some queer
way, was intimately concerned in the web in
which she and Zara seemed to be caught.

She couldn't pretend to explain, even to herself, the manner in which he might be affected,

but of the main fact she was sure. She knew that her memory had not deceived her; she had seen the man in Hedgeville. And the fact that he had deliberately lied about that seemed to her good evidence that he had something to conceal.

He knew Farmer Weeks. And in some fashion Farmer Weeks was intimately bound up with the affairs of Zara and her father. Everything that had happened since their flight from Hedgeville proved that beyond the shadow of a doubt. He had run great risks to get Zara back; although he was such a notorious miser, he had spent a good deal of money. And he was mixed up with Brack.

Suddenly a thought came to Bessie. Zara's father! He must know. And if he did, wasn't there a chance that he might be willing to talk to her, if she could only manage to see him? He distrusted Charlie Jamieson evidently, since he had refused to talk to him just when the lawyer had been sure that he was going to get some facts that would throw light on the mystery. But with Bessie he might well take a different stand. He had seen her in the country; he knew that she was a friend of Zara.

"Miss Eleanor," said Bessie, quickly, "I've got an idea and I wish you would let me talk to Mr. Jamieson about it. Will you, please—and by myself? You're angry still at Zara and her father, and perhaps you'd think I was all wrong."

"I'm not exactly angry, Bessie," said Eleanor. "I was hurt, but I'm beginning to see that very likely I am wrong, and that they were honestly mistaken, not deliberately ungrateful. At any rate, if Charlie Jamieson can stand the way Zara's father treats him, I guess I don't need to worry about it."

"Then may I go?"

"Yes, and hurry, or you'll find that he's left his office. You won't be long, will you?"

"No, indeed; only a few minutes. Will you be here in this store, Miss Eleanor, when I come back?"

"Yes, I'll meet you at the ribbon counter."

"Thank you, thank you ever so much, Miss Eleanor! I'll hurry just as much as I can, and I certainly won't be long."

Then she was off, and luckily enough she found that the lawyer had not yet gone. He listened to her suggestion with a smile.

"By George," he said, when she had finished, "maybe you've hit the right idea, Bessie, at that! I'm afraid I can't manage it today, but I'll take you to the jail myself in the morning, and see that you get a chance to talk to him. I doubt if he'll say anything, he's either obstinate or badly frightened. But it's worth the chance, if you don't mind going to the jail to see him. It's not a very nice place, you know."

Bessie laughed.

"I'd do worse than that if I thought I could help Zara, Mr. Jamieson," she said. "Do you know I've got the strangest feeling that she's in trouble? It's just as if I could hear her calling me and as if she were sorry for leaving us, and wanted to be back."

Jamieson smiled grimly.

"I think the chances are that she's feeling just about that way," he said. "She certainly ought to be—if we're at all near to guessing the people she's gone with. They won't treat her as well as the Mercers, I'll be bound."

"That's what I'm afraid of, too," said Bessie.

Then thanking him for his promise she made her way to the street, and started to go back to the store where she had left Eleanor. But she was intercepted. And, to her amazement, the person who checked her, as she was walking swiftly along the crowded street, was Jake Hoover.

"'Lo, Bessie," he said shamefacedly, as she started with surprise at the sight of him. "Say, you're pretty in them new clothes of your'n. I'd never 'a' known you."

"I wish you hadn't, then," said Bessie, with spirit. "I'm through with you, Jake Hoover! You won't have me around home any more, to take the blame for all your wickedness. When

things happen now they'll know whose fault it is
—and maybe they'll begin to think that you may
have done some of the things I used to get punished for, too.''

"Aw, now, don't get mad, Bessie,'' he said,
trying to pacify her. "This here's the city—
'tain't Hedgeville! Maybe I was mean to you
sometimes back home, Bessie, but I was jest
jokin'. Say, Bess, here's a gentleman wants to
talk to you. He's a lawyer an' a mighty smart
man. An' he thinks he knows somethin' about
your father and mother.''

Another figure had loomed up beside that of
Jake, and Bessie was hardly surprised to find that
it was Brack who was leering at her.

"He's right. I know something about them,''
he said. "There's precious little old Brack don't
know, my dear—an' that's a fact you can bet
your last dollar on.''

He chuckled, and made a movement as if he
intended to take Bessie's hand, but she brushed
his claw-like hand away with a motion of disgust.

"I haven't got time to be talking to you now,"
she said, decisively. "If you know anything you
think I ought to be told, tell it to Mr. Jamieson."

"Oh, ho, tell it to him, eh?" he said. "Maybe
you'd better be careful, girl! Maybe you
wouldn't like everyone to know why your parents
had to run away and leave you in such a hurry.
Maybe they're in prison, and deserve to be.
How'd you like to have people hear that, eh?"

"I wouldn't like it, but I don't believe it's
true!" said Bessie, scornfully. "Not for a
minute!" And she pressed on, but Brack followed and walked close beside her.

"Remember this—you'll never see them again,
except through me," he said, malevolently.

CHAPTER VII

OFF TO THE FARM

The next morning Bessie was doomed to be disappointed. She had looked forward confidently to seeing Zara's father, and had come to believe that there was a good chance for her to clear away some of the mystery that hung so heavily over Zara's affairs, even though she made no great progress toward straightening out her own confused ideas regarding herself and the reason for the disappearance of her parents. But, instead of the telephone call to Jamieson's office, for which she had waited with poorly concealed impatience from breakfast until nearly noon, she had a visit from Jamieson himself. The lawyer looked discouraged.

"Bad news, Bessie," he said, as soon as he saw her. She was waiting for him on the porch, and her eyes lighted with eagerness as soon as she saw him coming. "They've stolen a march on me."

"Why, how do you mean? Won't I be able to see Zara's father, after all?"

"Not just yet. Brack is cleverer than I thought. He's got a lot of political pull, and he got hold of a judge I thought was above stooping to anything wrong. So he was able to get this judge to sign an order putting him in my place as lawyer for Zara's father. The only way you can see the prisoner now is for Brack to give you permission, and if I know Brack, that's the last thing he'll do."

Bessie showed her discouragement.

"I'm afraid you're right there," she said. "I saw him yesterday, after I left you."

"You did? Whew! There's something queer here, Bessie. Now, try to remember just what was said and tell me all about it."

It was not hard for Bessie, guided by a few questions from Jamieson, to do that, and in a few moments she had supplied him with a complete review of her interview with the shyster, Brack. He nodded approvingly when she had finished.

"You did just right," he said, cheerfully. "I guess Mr. Brack won't get much change out of you, Bessie. There's one thing sure, you managed to acquire a lot of sense while you lived in Hedgeville. The sort we call common sense, though I don't know why, because it's the rarest sort of sense there is. Keep on acting just like that when people ask you questions and try to get you to tell them things."

"Do you think anyone else is likely to do that, Mr. Jamieson?"

"You can't tell. I'm all in the dark, you see. This thing acts just like a Chinese puzzle. They're simple enough when you know how to fit the pieces together, and you wonder why they ever stumped you. But until you do guess them—" He stopped, with a comical shrug of his shoulders to indicate his helplessness and his bewilderment, and Bessie laughed.

Then Eleanor came out, and the story of Brack's shrewdness had to be told to her.

"What are you going to do now?" she asked.

Jamieson threw up his hands with a laugh.

"Wait—and keep my eyes open," he said. "I'm going to act as if I'd lost all interest in the case. That may fool Brack. Our best chance now, you see, is to wait for the other side to make a mistake. They've made some already; the chances are they'll do it again. Then we can nab them. What I want to do is to make them think they're quite safe, that they needn't be afraid of us any more."

"You won't need Bessie, then, right away?"

"No. Really, she worries me. I feel as if she weren't safe here. They seem to be afraid of her, and I wouldn't put it past them to try to get hold of her and keep her where she can't do any talking until they've done what they want to do."

"But, Charlie, they must know that she's told us everything she knows already. Why should they want to take her away now?"

"If I knew that I could answer a lot of other questions, too. But here's a guess. Suppose she knows something without knowing at all what it means, or how important it is? That might easily be. She might be able to clear up the whole mystery with some single, seemingly unimportant remark. They may have good reason to know she hasn't done it yet, but they may also be afraid that, at any time, she will entirely by accident give away their whole game. And I've got an idea that if their game ever is exposed, someone will be in danger of going to jail. See? I'd like to figure out some good safe place for Bessie, where she'd be out of the way of all their tricks."

Eleanor clapped her hands.

"Then I've got the very place!" she said. "This business has upset the plans I'd made, but now I'm going to take my Camp Fire Girls down to dad's farm in Cheney County. You laughed at me when I was made a Camp Fire Guardian, Charlie, but you're going to see now what a fine thing the movement is."

"I didn't mean to laugh at you, Eleanor," he said, contritely. "And I got over doing it long ago, anyhow. I used to think this Camp Fire thing was a joke—just something got up to please a lot of girls who wanted to wear khaki skirts and camp out because their brothers had joined the Boy Scouts and told them what a good time they were having."

"That's just like a man," said Eleanor, quietly triumphant. "None of you think girls can do anything worth while on their own account. The Camp Fire Girls didn't imitate the Boy Scouts, and they're not a bit like them, really. We haven't anything against the Boy Scouts, but we think we're going to do better work among girls than even the Scout movement does among boys. Well, anyhow, we're going down to the farm, and Bessie shall go along. If anyone tries to kidnap her while she's with the girls, they'll have a hard time. We stick together, let me tell you, and Wohelo means something."

"You needn't preach to me, Eleanor," said the

lawyer, laughing. "You converted me long ago.
I'll stand for anything you do, anyhow. You're
all right—you've got more sense than most
men. It's a pity there aren't more girls like
you."

"That's rank flattery, and it isn't true, anyhow," laughed Eleanor. "But if I am any better than I used to be, it's because I've learned
not to think of myself first all the time. That's
what the Camp Fire teaches us, you see. Work,
and Health, and Love, that's what Wohelo means.
And it means to work for others, and to love
others, and to bring health to others as well as
to yourself. Come down to the farm while we're
there, and you'll see how it works out."

Jamieson got up.

"I probably will," he said, smiling as he held
out his hand in farewell. "I'll have to come
down to consult my client, you see."

"And you'll let us know if there's any news
of Zara, Mr. Jamieson, won't you?" said Bessie.
"I love the idea of going to the farm, but I rather

hate to leave the city when I don't know what may be happening to Zara.''

"You can't help her by staying here," said the lawyer, earnestly. "I'm quite sure of that. And I really think she's all right, and that she's being properly treated. After all, it's pretty hard to carry a girl like Zara off and keep her a prisoner against her will. It would be much better policy to treat her well, and keep her contented. It's quite plain that she thought she was going with friends when she went, or she would have made some sort of a row. And their best policy is to keep her quiet.''

"But they didn't act that way before we got away from Hedgeville—clear away, I mean," said Bessie. "Farmer Weeks caught her in the road, you know, and locked her in that room the time that I followed her and helped her to get away through the woods.''

"Yes, but that was a very different matter, Bessie. In that state Weeks had the law on his side. The court was ready to name him as her guardian, and to bind her over to him until she was twenty-one. In this state neither he nor anyone else, except her father, has any more right to keep her from going where she likes than they have to tell me what I must do—as long as we obey the law and don't do anything that is wrong.''

"Then you think she's well and happy?"

"I'm quite sure of it," said Jamieson heartily. "This isn't some foreign country. It's America, where there are plenty of people to notice anything that seems wrong or out of the ordinary. And if they were treating Zara badly, she'd be pretty sure to find someone who would help her to get away."

"Yes, this is America," said Bessie, thoughtfully. "But you see, Zara has lived in countries where things are very different. And maybe she doesn't know her rights. After all, you know, she thinks her father hasn't done anything wrong, and still she's seen him put in prison and kept there. What I'm afraid of is that

2—C8

she'll get to think that this is just like the countries she knows best, and be afraid to do anything, or try to get help, no matter what they
do.''

"Well, we mustn't borrow trouble," said Jamieson, frowning slightly at the thoughts Bessie's
words suggested to him. "We can't do anything
more now, that's sure. Have a good time, and
stop worrying. That's the best legal advice I
can give you right now."

Once her mind was made up, Eleanor acted
quickly. The outing at her father's farm, which
was not at all like the Hoover farm in Hedgeville of which Bessie King had such unpleasant
memories, was one that had long been promised
to her girls, and she herself had been looking
forward to going there. The troubles of Bessie
and Zara had almost led her to abandon the idea
of going there herself, and she had arranged for
a friend to take her place as Guardian for a
time. Now, however, she sent word to all her
girls, and that very evening they met at the sta-

tion and took the train for Deer Crossing, the little station that was nearest to the farm.

"They'll meet us in the farm wagons," said Eleanor, when the girls were all aboard. "So we'll have a ride through the moonlight to the farm—the moon rises early to-night, you know."

It was a jolly, happy ride in the train, and Bessie, renewing her acquaintance with the Camp Fire Girls, who had seemed to her and Zara, when they had first seen them, like creatures from another world, felt her depression wearing off. They had a car to themselves, thanks to the conductor, who had known Eleanor Mercer since she was a little girl, and as the train sped through the country scenes that were so familiar to Bessie, the girls laughed and talked and sang songs of the Camp Fire, and made happy plans for walks and tramps in the country about the farm.

"It's just like the country around Hedgeville, Miss Eleanor," said Bessie, as the Guardian stopped beside the seat she shared with her first chum among the Camp Fire Girls, Minnehaha.

"The houses look the same, and the stone fences, and—oh, everything!"

"I wonder if you aren't a little bit homesick, down in your heart, Bessie?" laughed Miss Mercer. "Come, now, confess!"

"Perhaps I am," said Bessie, wonderingly. "I never thought of that. But it's just for the country, and the cows and the animals, and all the things I'm used to seeing. I wouldn't go back to Maw Hoover's for anything."

"You shan't, Bessie. I was only joking," said Eleanor, quickly. "I know just how you feel. I've been that way myself. When you get away from a place you begin very quickly to forget everything that was disagreeable that happened there, and you only remember the good times you had. That's why you're homesick."

"We'll be able to take walks and go for straw rides here, won't we, Wanaka?" asked Minnehaha. She used Eleanor's fire name, Wanaka, just as Minnehaha was her fire name; her own was Margery Burton.

"You'll have to, if you expect to be in fashion," laughed the Guardian. "And you shall learn to milk cows and find eggs and do all sorts of farm work, too. I expect Bessie will want to laugh often at you girls. You see, she knows all about that sort of thing, and you'll all be terrible green-horns, I think."

"I ought to know about a farm," said Bessie. "I lived on one long enough. And I don't see why I should laugh at the rest of the girls. They know more about the city now than I ever will know. I've been there long enough to find that out, anyhow."

Just then the conductor put his head inside the door, and called "Deer Crossing!"

As the train slowed up, all the girls made a rush for their bags and bundles, and five minutes later they were standing and watching the dis-appearing train, waving to the amused conductor and trainmen, who were all on the platform of the last car. Then the train disappeared around a curve, and they had a chance to devote their

attention to the two big farm wagons that were
waiting near the station, each with its team of
big Percherons and its smiling driver. The
drivers were country boys, with fair, tousled hair,
and both wore neat black suits. At the sight of
them Eleanor burst into a laugh.

"Why, Sid Harris—and you, too, Walter
Stubbs!" she cried. "This isn't Sunday! What
are you doing in your store clothes, just as if
you were on your way to church?"

Both the boys flushed and neither of them had
a word to say.

"Did you get mixed up on the days of the
week?" Eleanor went on, pitilessly.

All the girls were enjoying their confusion, and
black-eyed Dolly Ransom, the tease of the party,
laughed aloud.

"I bet they never saw so many girls together
before, Miss Eleanor," she said, with a toss of
her pretty head. "That's why they're so quiet!
They probably don't have girls in the country."

"Don't they, just!" said Eleanor, laughing

back at her. "Wait until you see them, Dolly. They'll put your nose out of joint, the girls around here. If you think you're going to have it all your own way with the boys out here, the way you do so much at home, you're mistaken."

Dolly tossed her head again. She looked at the confused, blushing boys on the wagons, who could hardly be expected to understand that Dolly was only teasing them, and wanted nothing better than a perfectly harmless flirtation.

"They're welcome to boys like those," she said, airily. "I'll wait until I get home, Miss Eleanor."

Then she turned away, and Eleanor, her face serious for a moment, turned to Bessie.

"She'll wait until she's grown up, too, if I've got anything to say about it," she said. "Bessie, when Zara comes back, of course you'll be with her mostly. But I wish you'd make a friend of Dolly Ransom,—a real friend. Her mother's dead, and she has no sisters."

"I hope I can," said Bessie, simply. "I like her ever so much."

CHAPTER VIII

A NEW CHUM

The farm was nearly five miles from the station, and the two big wagons made slow time with the heavy loads, especially as the roads were still muddy from a recent downpour. But none of the Camp Fire Girls seemed to mind the length of the trip.

Now that she was actually out in the heart of it, Bessie found that the country was not as much like that around Hedgeville as it had seemed to be from the train windows. The fields were better kept; there were no unpainted, dilapidated looking houses, such as those of Farmer Weeks and some of the other neighbors of the Hoovers in Hedgeville whom she remembered so well.

Neat fences, well kept up, marked off the fields, and, even to Bessie's eyes, although she was far from being an agricultural expert, the crops

121

themselves looked better. She spoke of this to Eleanor.

"These aren't just ordinary farms," Eleanor explained. "My father and some other men who have plenty of money have bought up a lot of land around here, and they are working the farms, and making them pay just as much as possible. My father thinks it's a shame for so many boys and young men, whose fathers own farms, to go rushing off to the city and work in stores and factories. And they started out to find out why it was that way. They're business men, you see, and as soon as they really began to think about it they found out what was wrong."

"Why the boys went to the city?" asked Bessie. "I should think that would be easy to see! It was around Hedgeville. Why, on a farm, the work never is done. It's work all day, and then get up before daylight to start again. And even Paw Hoover, who had a good farm, was always saying how poor he was, and how he wished he could make more money."

"I'll bet he was always buying new land, though," said Eleanor, looking wise.

"Yes, he was," admitted Bessie. "He always said that if he could get enough land he'd be rich."

"He probably had too much as it was, Bessie. The trouble with most farmers is that they don't know how to use the land they have, instead of that they haven't enough. They don't treat the soil right, and they won't spend money for good farm machinery and for rich fertilizers. If they did that, and studied farming, the way men study to be doctors or lawyers, they'd be better off. How many acres did Paw Hoover have? Well, it doesn't matter, but I'll bet that my father gets more out of one acre on his farm than Paw Hoover does out of two on his. You see, the man who's in charge of the farm went to college to study the business, and he knows all sorts of things that make a farm pay better."

"Paw Hoover was talking about that once, saying he wished he could send Jake to college to study farming. But Maw laughed at him, and

Jake couldn't have gone, anyhow. He was so stupid that he never even got through school there in Hedgeville.''

"I suppose he is stupid," said Eleanor. "But after all, Bessie, when a boy doesn't get along well in school it doesn't always mean that it's his fault. He may not be properly taught. Sometimes it's the school's fault, and not the pupil's.''

"Other people got along all right," said Bessie. She wasn't quite prepared to say a good word for Jake Hoover yet. He had caused her too much trouble in the past.

"Why," she went on, "I used to have to do his lessons for him all the time. He just wouldn't study at home, Miss Eleanor, and in school he was so big, and such a bully, that most of the teachers were afraid of him.''

"That just shows they weren't good teachers, Bessie. No good teacher is ever afraid of a bully. She has plenty of people to back her up if she really needs help. I don't say Jake Hoover is any better than he ought to be, but from all you tell me, part of his trouble may be because he hasn't been properly handled. But let's forget him, anyhow. Look over there. Do you see that white house on top of the hill?"

"Against the sun, so that it's sort of pink where the sun strikes it?" said Bessie. "Yes, what a lovely place!"

"Well, that's where we're going," said Eleanor.

"But—but that doesn't look a bit like a farmhouse!" said Bessie, surprised. "I thought—"

"You thought it would be more like the Hoover farm, didn't you?" laughed Eleanor. "Well, of course that's only our house, and Dad built a nice one, on the finest piece of land he could find, because we were going to spend a good deal of time there. There's electric light and running water in all the rooms and we're just as comfortable there as we would be in the city."

"It's beautiful, but really, Miss Eleanor, I

don't believe most farmers could afford a place like that, even if they were a lot better off than Paw Hoover—"

"They could afford a lot of the comforts, Bessie, because they don't cost half as much as you'd think. The electric light, for instance, and the running water. The light comes from power that we get from the brook right on the farm, and it costs less than it does to light the house in the city. And the water is pumped from the well by a windmill that cost very little to put up. You see, there's a big tank on the roof, and whenever there's a wind, the mill is started to running and the tank is filled. Then there's enough water on hand to last even if there shouldn't be enough wind to turn the mill for two or three days, though that's something that very seldom happens. If all the farmers knew how easily they could have these little comforts, and how cheap they are, I believe more of them would put in those conveniences."

"Oh, how much easier it would have been at

Hoover's if we'd had them!" sighed Bessie. "There we had to fill the lamps every day, and every bit of water we used in the house had to be drawn at the well and carried in pails. It was awfully hard work."

"You see, Maw Hoover didn't have such an easy time, Bessie," said Eleanor. "She had all that work about the house to do for years and years. She didn't need to be so mean to you, but, after all, she might have been nicer if she'd had a pleasanter life. It's easy to be nice and agreeable when everything is easy, and everything goes right, but when you have to work hard all the time, if you're a little bit inclined to be mean, the grind of doing the same thing day after day, year after year, seems to bring the meanness right out. I've seen lots of instances of that, and I'm perfectly sure that if I were a farmer's wife, and had to work like a slave I'd be a perfect shrew and there'd be no living with me at all."

They turned in from the road now, the wagon

in which Bessie and Eleanor rode in the lead, and came into a pretty avenue that led up a gentle grade to the ridge on which the house was built. There were trees at each side to provide shade in the hot part of the day, and for a long distance on each side of the trees there were well kept lawns.

"My father likes a place to be beautiful as well as useful," said Eleanor, "so he had those lawns made when we built the house. All the farmers in the neighborhood thought it was an awful waste of good land, but since then some of them have come to see that if they ever wanted to sell their places people would like them better if they were pretty, and they've copied this place a good deal in the neighborhood.

"We're very glad, because right now Cheney County is the prettiest farming section anywhere around, and the crops are about the best in the state, too. So, you see, we seem to have shown them that they can have pretty places and still make money. And sometimes those lawns are used for grazing sheep, so they're useful as well as ornamental.''

Then in a few minutes they were at the house, and the smiling housekeeper, whom Eleanor introduced to the girls as Mrs. Farnham, greeted them.

"Come right in," she said, heartily. "There's supper ready and waiting—fried chicken, and corn bread, and honey, and creamed potatoes, and fresh milk, and apple pie and—"

"Stop, stop, do, Mrs. Farnham!" pleaded Eleanor. "You'll make me so hungry that I won't want to wash my hands!"

And the supper, when they came to it, was just as good to taste as it was to hear about. Everything they ate, it seemed, came from the farm. No store goods were ever used on the table in that house. And Bessie, used to a farm where chickens, except when they were old and tough, were never eaten, but kept for sale, wondered at the goodness of everything.

That night, although it was not part of the plan, there was an informal camp fire, held about

2—C9

a blazing pyre of logs. But it did not last long, for everyone was tired and ready indeed for the signal that Eleanor gave early by lifting her voice in the notes of the good-night song, *Lay Me to Sleep in Sheltering Flame.*

Bessie, rather to her surprise, found that she was not to room with Margery Burton, or Minnehaha, as she had expected, but was to share a big room, under the roof, with Dolly Ransom, the merry, michievous Kiama, as she was known to her comrades of the fire.

"Do you mind if I snore?" asked Dolly promptly, when they were alone together. "Because I probably shall, and everyone makes such a fuss, and acts as if it was my fault."

"I'm so tired I shan't even hear you," said Bessie, with a laugh. "Snore all you like, I won't mind!"

Dolly looked surprised, and pouted a little.

"If you don't mind, there's no use doing it," she said, after a moment, and Bessie laughed again at this unconscious confession.

"I thought you couldn't help it," she said, with a smile.

Dolly looked a little confused.

"I can't sometimes, when I've got a cold," she said. "But they go on so about it then that I have sometimes tried to do it, just to get even."

"You're a tease, Kiama," said Bessie, merrily, "and I guess it's that that you can't help. But go ahead and try to tease me as much as you like. I won't mind."

"Then I won't do it," decided Dolly, suddenly. "It's fun teasing people when they get mad, but what's the use when they think it's a joke?"

Bessie had seen little of Dolly in the first days of her acquaintance with the Manasquan Camp Fire, but now, as they appraised one another, knowing that they were to be very intimate during their stay on the farm, Bessie decided that she was going to like her new friend very much.

Not as much as Zara, probably—that would be natural, for Zara was Bessie's first chum, and her best, and Bessie's loyalty was one of her chief traits. But she was not the sort of a girl who can have only one friend. Usually girls who say that mean that they can have only one close friend at a time, and what happens is that they have innumerable chums, each of whom seems to be the best while the friendship lasts. Bessie wanted to be friendly with everyone, and what Eleanor had begun to tell her about Dolly made her think that perhaps the mischief maker of the Camp Fire was lonely like herself.

"You're just like me—you haven't any mother or sister, have you?" said Dolly, after they were both in bed.

Bessie was glad of the darkness that hid the quick flush that stained her cheeks. Since she had talked with Brack she was beginning to feel that there was something shameful about her position, although, had she stopped to think, she would have known that no one who knew the facts would blame her, even if her parents had behaved badly in deserting her. And, as a matter of fact, Bessie clung to the belief that her parents had not acted of their own free will in leaving her so long with the Hoovers. She thought, and meant to keep on thinking, that they had been unable to help themselves, and that some time, when good fortune came to them again, she would see them and that they would make up to her in love for all the empty, unhappy years in Hedgeville.

"Yes, I'm like you, Dolly," she answered, finally. "I don't know what's become of my parents. I wish I did."

"I know what's become of mine," said Dolly, her voice suddenly hard—too hard for so young a girl. "My mother's dead. She died when I was a baby. And my father doesn't care what becomes of me. He lives in Europe, and once in a while he sends me money but he doesn't seem to want to see me, ever."

"Where do you live, Dolly?" asked Bessie.

"Oh, with my Aunt Mabel," said Dolly. "You'll see her when we go back to town for

I'm going to have you come and visit me if you
will. She's an old maid, and she's terribly
proper, and if ever I start to have any fun she
thinks it must be wicked, and tries to make me
stop. But I fool her—you just bet I do!''

They were quiet for a minute, and then Dolly
broke out again.

"I don't believe Aunt Mabel ever was young!''
she said fiercely. "She doesn't act as if she'd
ever been a girl. And she seems to think I ought
to be just as sober and quiet as if I were her
age—and she's fifty! Isn't that dreadful,
Bessie?''

"I think you'd have a hard time acting as if
you were fifty, Dolly,'' said Bessie, honestly, and
trying to suppress a laugh but in vain. "You
don't, do you?''

"Of course not!'' said Dolly, giggling frankly,
and seemingly not at all hurt because Bessie did
not take the recital of her troubles more seriously.
"Aunt Mabel would like you. I don't mean that
you're stiff and priggish like her, but you seem

quieter than most of the girls, and more serious minded. I bet you like school."

"I do," laughed Bessie. "But I like vacations too, don't you? This is the first time I ever really had one, though. I've always had to work harder in summer than in winter before this."

"I think that's dreadful, Bessie. Listen! You know all about farms, don't you? Let's go off by ourselves to-morrow and explore, shall we?"

"Maybe," said Bessie. "We'll see what we're supposed to do."

"All right! I'm sleepy, too. Bother what we're supposed to do, Bessie! Let's do what we like. This is vacation, and you're supposed to do what you like in vacation time. So you see it's all right, anyhow. We can do what we like and what we're supposed to do both. That's the way it ought always to be, I think."

"They'd say we ought to want to do what we're supposed to do, you know, Dolly. That's the safe way. Then you can't go wrong."

"Well—but do you always want to do what you're supposed to do?"

"I'm afraid not. Good-night!"

"Good-night!"

CHAPTER IX

Breakfast on the farm was just such another meal as supper had been. Again Bessie wondered at the profusion of good things that, at the Hoovers, had always been kept for sale instead of being used on the table. There was rich, thick cream, for instance, fresh fruit and all sorts of good things, so that anyone whose whole acquaintance with country fare was confined to what the Mercer farm provided might well have believed all the tales of the good food of the farm. Bessie knew, of course, without ever having thought much about it, that on many American farms, despite the ease with which fresh fruits and vegetables are to be had, a great deal of canned stuff is used.

"Bessie," said Eleanor, after breakfast, "this is rather different from the Hoovers, isn't it?"

"It certainly is," agreed Bessie.

137

"Well, of course it isn't possible right now,
Bessie, but I've been thinking that some time,
when Maw Hoover has gotten over her dislike
for you, you may be able to teach her and some
of the other farm women in Hedgeville how much
more pleasant their lives could be."

Bessie looked surprised.

"Why, I don't believe I'll ever dare go back
there," she said. "I believe Maw Hoover would
be willing to put me in prison if she could for
setting that barn on fire. I'm sure she thinks I
did it. She wouldn't believe it was Jake, with
his silly trick of trying to frighten me with those
burning sticks."

"She'll find out the truth some time, Bessie,
never fear. And think about what I said. One
of the great things this Camp Fire movement
is trying to do is to make women's lives healthier
and happier all over the country. And I don't
believe that we've thought half enough of the
women on the farms so far. You've made me
realize that."

"But there are lots and lots of Camp Fires in country places, aren't there, Miss Eleanor? I read about ever so many of them."

"Yes, but not in the sort of country places I mean. There are Camp Fires, and plenty of them, in the towns in the country, and even in the bigger villages. But the places I'm thinking of are those like Hedgeville, where all the village there is is just a post office and two or three stores, where the people come in from the farms for miles around to get their mail and buy a few things. You know how much good a Camp Fire would do in Hedgeville, but it would be pretty hard to get one started."

Bessie's eyes shone.

"Oh, I wish there was one!" she cried. "I know lots of the girls on the farms there would love to do the things we do. They're nice girls, lots of them, though they didn't like me much. You see, Jake Hoover used to tell his maw lies about me, and she told them to her friends, and they told their girls—and they believed them, of course. I think that was one reason why I couldn't get along very well with the other girls."

"I think that's probably the real reason, Bessie, just as you say. But if you go back you can make it different, I'm sure. You needn't be afraid of Jake Hoover any more, I think, especially after what he did at General Seeley's."

"Killing that poor pheasant? Wasn't that a mean thing for him to do? They used to say he did some poaching, sometimes, around Hedgeville, but then about everyone did there, I guess. But I didn't think he'd ever try to catch such beautiful birds as the ones General Seeley had."

"I could forgive him for killing the bird much more easily than for trying to get you blamed for doing it, Bessie. But let's change the subject. How did you and Dolly Ransom get along?"

Bessie smiled at the recollection of the stream of questions she had had to answer from her new roommate.

"She's great!" she said, enthusiastically. "I

think we're going to be fine friends, Miss Eleanor.''

"I hope so. There isn't a bit of real harm in Dolly, but she's mischievous and loves to tease, and I'm afraid that some time she'll go too far and get herself into trouble without meaning to at all.''

"She doesn't like her aunt, Miss Eleanor— the one she lives with now that her father's away so much.''

Miss Mercer made a wry face.

"Miss Ransom's lovely in many ways,'' she said, "but she doesn't understand young girls, and she seems to think that Dolly ought to be just as wise and staid and sober as if she were grown up. I think that is the chief reason for Dolly's mischief. It has to have some way to escape, and she's pretty well tied down at home. So I overlook a lot of her tricks, when, if one of the other girls was guilty, I'd have to speak pretty severely about it. Well, here she is now! Go off with her if you like, Bessie.''

"Oh, Miss Mercer, what do we have to do this morning?" shouted Dolly as soon as she saw Bessie and the Guardian.

"What you like until after lunch, Dolly. Then perhaps we may want to arrange to do something all together—have a cooking lesson, or learn something about the farm. We'll see. But you and Bessie might as well go over the place now and get acquainted with it. Bessie can probably find her way about easier than you city girls."

"Oh, I'm so glad!" cried Dolly. "Come on, Bessie! I bet we can have lots of sport."

So they went off, and, though Bessie wanted to see the great barn in which the horses were kept, Dolly wanted to go toward the road at the entrance of the place, and Bessie yielded, since the choice of direction didn't seem a bit important then.

"I saw one of those boys who drove us up last night going off this way," Dolly explained, guilelessly, "and, Bessie, he looked ever so much

nicer in his blue overalls than he did in that
horrible, stiff, black suit he was wearing last
night.''

"You shouldn't laugh at his clothes. They're
his very best, Dolly. The overalls are just his
working clothes, and you'd hurt his feelings terribly if he knew that you were laughing at the
store clothes. He probably had to save up his
money for a long time to buy them.''

"Oh, well, I don't care! I wonder if there's
any place around here where you can buy ice-
cream soda? I'm just dying to have some.''

"I thought you were going without soda and
candy for a month to get an honor bead, Dolly.''

"Oh, bother! I was, but it was too hard. I
got a soda when I'd gone without for two weeks,
and I never thought of the old honor bead until
I'd begun to drink it. So that discouraged me,
and I gave it up.''

"But don't you feel much better when you
don't eat candy and drink sodas between
meals?''

"I don't know—maybe I do. Yes, I guess I do. But they taste so good, Bessie!"

"Well, I'm afraid you'll have to do without the soda here."

Dolly was still really leading the way, and now, her eyes on a blue clad figure, she decided to leave the avenue of trees that led to the road and cut across a field.

"Don't you love the smell of hay, Bessie?" asked Dolly. "I think it's fine. That's one of the things I like best about the country, and being on a farm."

"I guess I know it too well to get excited about it, Dolly. You see, I've lived on a farm almost all my life, and so things like that aren't new to me. But it is lovely and, yes, I do believe I've missed it, there in the city."

"Wouldn't you rather live in the city, though?"

"Yes, because I wasn't happy where I was in the country, and in the city I've had everything to make me happy. I suppose you'd rather live in the country, though?"

"No, indeed! I like to hear the city noises at night, and to see all the people. And I like to go to the theatre, when my aunt lets me go to a matinee, and to the moving picture shows, and everything like that. Don't you love the movies?"

"I never went, so I don't know."

"Not really? You don't mean they haven't even got a moving picture place in Hedgeville? I never heard of such a thing!"

Bessie laughed.

"Moving pictures are pretty new, Dolly. No one could go to them until a little while ago, no matter where they lived, or how much money they had. And I guess people got along all right without them."

"Yes, but they had to get along without lots of things until they were invented—telephones and electric lights, and lots and lots of useful things like that. But you wouldn't expect us to get along without them now, would you?"

"I guess it's only the things we know about that we really need, Dolly. If we don't know

2—C10

about a lot of these modern things, we keep right
along getting on without them.   Like Hedgeville—the only man there who has a telephone
is Farmer Weeks.''

"Yes," said Dolly triumphantly, "and he's got
more money than all the rest of the people in
the place put together, hasn't he?''

Bessie laughed.

"And all this just because you want an ice-
cream soda!   What will you do if you really
can't have one, Dolly?''

"I don't know!   I'm just hankering for one—
my mouth is watering from thinking about it!''

"We might ask this boy.   Miss Eleanor said
his name was Stubbs, Walter Stubbs.''

Bessie smiled to herself as she saw how surprised Dolly was trying to seem at the discovery
that they had come to the part of the field where
Walter was working.   He was red to the ears,
but Bessie could tell from the way he was looking at Dolly that the city girl, with her smart
clothes and her pretty face, had already made a

deep impression on the farm boy. Now, as the
two girls approached, he looked at them sheep-
ishly, standing first on one foot, then on the
other.

"Do you work all the time?" Dolly asked him,
impishly, darting a look at Bessie.

"Cal'late to—most of the time," said Walter.

"Don't you ever have any fun? Don't you
ever meet a couple of girls and treat them to
ice-cream soda, for instance?"

"Oh, sure!" said Walter. "Year ago come
October Si Hinkle an' I, we went to the city for
the day with the gals we was buzzin' then an'
we bought 'em each an ice-cream sody."

"Did you have to go to the city to do that?"
said Dolly.

"Sure! Ain't no place nigher'n that. Over
to Deer Crossin' there's a man has lemon pop in
bottles sometimes, but he ain't got no founting
like we saw in the city, nor no ice-cream, neither."

Dolly was a picture of woe and disappointment.

"Tell yer what, though," said Walter, bashfully. "Saturday night there's a goin' to be an ice-cream festival over to the Methodist Church at the Crossing, an' I'm aimin' ter go, though my folks is Baptists. I'll treat yer to a plate of ice-cream over there."

"Will you, really?" said Dolly, brightening up and looking as pleased as if the ice-cream soda she wanted so much had suddenly been set down before her in the field.

"I sure will," said Walter, hugely pleased. "Say, they play all sorts of games over there—forfeits an' post office an'—"

Bessie had to laugh at Dolly's look of mystification.

"Come on, Dolly," she said. "We mustn't keep Walter from his work or he'll be getting into trouble. We can see him again some time when he isn't so busy." And as they walked off she told Dolly about the country games the boy had spoken of—games in which kissing played a large part.

"The country isn't as nice as I thought," said

Dolly dolefully. "I'm so thirsty, and there's no place to buy even sarsaparilla!"

"Maybe not, but I can show you something better than that for your thirst, Dolly. See that rocky place over there, under the trees? I'll bet there's a spring there. Let's find out."

Sure enough, there was a spring, carefully covered, and a cup, so that anyone working in the fields could get water, and even Dolly had to admit that no ice-cream soda had ever quenched her thirst as well.

"What delicious water!" she exclaimed. "Where's the ice?"

"There isn't any, silly!" laughed Bessie. "It's cold like that because it comes bubbling right up out of the ground."

"I bet that's just the sort of water they sell in bottles in the city, because it's so much purer than the city water," said Dolly. "But that's an awfully little spring, Bessie."

"The basin isn't very big, but that doesn't mean that there isn't always plenty of water.

You see, no matter how much you take out, there's always more coming. See that little brook? Well, this spring feeds that, and it runs off and joins other brooks, but there's always water here just the same. Of course, in a drought, if there was no rain for a long time, it might dry up, but it doesn't look as if that ever happened here.''

"Well, it is good water, and that's a lot better, than nothing," said Dolly. "Come on! We started for the road. Let's go down and sit on the fence and watch the people go by."

So they made their way on through the field until they came to the road, and there they sat on the fence, enjoying some apples that Bessie had pronounced eatable, after several attempts by Dolly to consume some from half a dozen trees that would have caused her a good deal of pain later. Two or three automobiles passed as they sat there, and Dolly looked at their occupants enviously.

"If we had a car, Bessie," she said, "we could

get to some place where they sell ice-cream soda
in no time, and be back in plenty of time for
lunch, too. I wish some friend of mine would
come along in one of those motors!''

None did, but, vastly to Bessie's surprise, they
had not been there long before a big green touring
car that had shot by them a few minutes before
so fast that they could not see its occupants at
all, came back, doubling on its course, and
stopped in the road just before them. And on
the driver's seat, discarding his goggles so that
Bessie could recognize him, was Mr. Holmes—
the man who had taken her and Miss Mercer for
a ride, and whom she felt she had so much
reason to distrust!

''This is good fortune! I'm very glad indeed
to see you,'' he said, cordially, to Bessie. ''Miss
King, is it not—Miss Bessie King, Miss Mercer's
friend? Won't you introduce me to the other
young lady?''

CHAPTER X

A FOOLISH PROCEEDING

Reluctantly enough, Bessie yielded to his request. If she had known how to avoid introducing Holmes to Dolly, she would have done it. But she was not old enough, and not experienced enough, to understand how to manage such an affair. Had there been occasion, Miss Eleanor, of course, could have snubbed a man and still been perfectly polite while she was doing it. But Bessie had not reached that point yet.

"Are you staying down here together? How very pleasant!" said Holmes. "This seems to be a beautiful place from the road, but of course one can't see very much from an automobile."

"We're down here with our Camp Fire—a lot of the girls," explained Dolly, hurriedly. "Miss Mercer is Guardian of the Camp Fire, and this is her father's farm. It is a nice place, but it's dreadfully slow. Just fancy, there isn't a place anywhere around where we can even get an ice-cream soda!''

"Dolly!" said Bessie, in a low voice, reproach-fully. "You mustn't—"

"What a tragedy!" said Holmes, laughing.

"Oh, of course, you don't know what it is to have a craving for soda and not be able to get it!" said Dolly, pouting. "So you laugh at me—"

Holmes was all regret in a moment.

"My dear Miss Dolly!" he protested. "I wasn't laughing at you at all—really I wasn't! I was smiling at the idea of there being such a primitive place in a civilized country. Really, I was! And I'm sure it is a tragedy. I believe I'm as fond of ice-cream soda as you, if I am such an old fellow. And, after all, though it seems so tragic, it's easily mended, you know. I happen to remember passing a most attractive looking drug store in a town about five miles back, and that's no ride at all in this car. Jump in, both of you, and I'll run you there and back in no time!''

"Oh, that's awfully kind of you, but I really think we shouldn't," stammered Dolly, who had meant, as soon as she saw that Holmes knew Bessie, to get that invitation.

"Of course we shouldn't, Dolly," said Bessie, irritated, since she saw through Dolly's rather transparent little scheme at once. "It's very kind of you, Mr. Holmes, but we mustn't think of troubling you so much. Dolly doesn't really want an ice-cream soda at all; she just thinks she does, and she's much better off without it."

"Oh, come, that's very unkind, Miss Bessie! I can see that your friend is really suffering for a strawberry ice-cream soda. And you mustn't talk as if I would be taking any trouble. I'm just riding around the country aimlessly, for want of something better to do. I'm not going anywhere in particular, and it doesn't matter when I get there or if I never get there at all. I'm just a useless man, too old to work any longer. Surely you won't refuse to let me make myself useful to a young lady in distress?"

"Oh," said Dolly. "Really, is that so, Mr. Holmes? Wouldn't it be a dreadful amount of trouble to you? Of course, if that's so, and you really want us to come—"

"Nonsense, Dolly!" said Bessie, severely. "We can't go, and we must be getting back to the house. Thank you ever so much, Mr. Holmes— and good-morning!"

But Dolly was not to be deprived of her treat so easily.

"I think you're very rude, Bessie!" she said, bridling. "That may be the proper way to act in the country where you came from, but it's not the way we do things in the city at all. Thank you very much, Mr. Holmes, and I shall be very pleased to accept your kind invitation, if you're sure it's not troubling you."

"There you are, Miss Bessie!" said Holmes, heartily. "Now, you won't be so unkind as to let Miss Dolly come with me alone, will you? She's coming, and I think you'd better change your mind and come, too."

Poor Bessie was in a quandary. She knew that Miss Mercer, even though she had laughed at her suspicions of Mr. Holmes, would not approve of such a prank as this; but she knew, also, that Dolly, inclined to be defiant and to resent the exercise of any authority, would not be moved by that argument. And, in the presence of Holmes, she could hardly tell Dolly the story of Zara's disappearance and her own suspicions concerning the part that Holmes, or, at least, his car, had played in it. Neither, she felt, could she let Dolly go alone. The chances were that Holmes meant no harm, but she knew that Miss Eleanor had put Dolly in her charge in a measure, and she felt responsible for her new chum.

So, displeased as she was, Bessie climbed into the car after Dolly, who had already taken her place in the tonneau, and in a moment they were off, taking the road that led away from Deer Crossing. Holmes only smiled as she got in the car, but before he put on his dust glasses Bessie was sure that she saw a look of triumph in his eyes, as if he had succeeded beyond his hopes in some plan he had formed. Bessie did not at all relish the prospect of the little adventure upon which Dolly's whim had launched her, but she decided to take it with a good grace, since, now that she was in the car, she had to see it through.

Once the car was under way, going fast, Mr. Holmes had to devote all his attention to driving, and, as it was a large one, there was so much noise the two girls could talk without being heard.

"I suppose you're awfully mad at me," said Dolly, in a whisper, looking at Bessie's stern face. "Oh, Bessie, I couldn't help it! He was so nice about it, and it was such a lovely chance to tease you! I do try to be good, but every time I see a chance to do anything like that I just can't seem to help it."

"I asked you not to. You could see I didn't want to go, Dolly. And if we're going to be friends, you oughtn't to force me into doing things I don't want to do."

"Oh, Bessie, you're not going to be mean about it, and keep on being angry? You won't tell Miss Eleanor, will you? She'd send me home—I know she would!"

"I won't tell her, and I'm not going to be angry, either, Dolly. But I'm very much afraid you'll be sorry yourself before we get back to the farm, and I don't see how Miss Eleanor can help finding out, because I'm pretty sure Mr. Holmes isn't going to get us back in time for lunch."

"Why, Bessie, he said he would—he promised! Don't you think he means to keep his word?"

"I hope so, Dolly, but he told me something once that wasn't so, and—oh, well, let's not worry about it now, anyhow. I can't explain everything to you now, there isn't time. It's a lovely ride, isn't it? We might as well enjoy ourselves, now that we're in for it."

"That's what I say, Bessie. There's no use crying over spilt milk, is there? And I guess it

will be all right. I think he's awfully nice. I
don't see why you don't like him."

"You will when you know as much as I do,
Dolly, I'm afraid. But we won't talk any more
about that. Oh, look, there is a town, right here!
We're coming into it now, do you see? Probably
this is the place Mr. Holmes meant he was going
to bring us to."

But Bessie's fears were redoubled a minute or
so later, when the car, without slackening speed
at all, shot through a street that was lined with
shops, two or three of which, as they could see,
were drug stores with ice-cream soda signs that
they could easily read even from the fast moving
car.

Looking at Bessie as if she were already a little
frightened and sorry, Dolly leaned over and
touched Mr. Holmes on the shoulder.

"Aren't you going to stop here?" she asked,
"I'm sure those are awfully nice looking stores,
Mr. Holmes."

He slowed up the car at once, and turned to
them with a pleasant smile.

"Oh, this isn't the place I meant at all," he said. "I don't know anything about the stores here. The place I was thinking of is much better, and it's not very far away. Besides, it's early yet, and I think we ought to have as much of a ride as we can, don't you?"

Dolly looked dubious. One glance at Bessie had shown her that her chum was not prepared to accept this explanation. But they had no choice, for Holmes, seeming to take their assent to his plan for granted, had turned on full power, and the car was roaring out into open country again, but now in a direction almost at right angles to its former course. They were traveling due west, and Bessie, without anything definite to alarm her, felt herself growing more and more nervous with the passing minutes. She felt that something was wrong.

Her distrust of Holmes, save for so much of it as was due to his statement that he had never been in Hedgeville, when she herself had seen him there, was almost wholly instinctive, but

2—C11

Bessie knew that instinct is sometimes a better guide than reason, and she began to regret Dolly's impulsive action in getting into the car more and more. Still, as matters stood, there was nothing to do but wait and see what was to happen.

After all, no matter what might come, she would not be utterly unprepared. She was expecting trouble of some sort, and she knew that the worst blows are those that are unexpected, just as the worst lightning is that which flashes from a clear sky.

Suddenly, as the car approached a little country store, at a crossroads, and looking as though no one ever went there to buy anything, Holmes slowed up again.

"This isn't the place you mean, is it?" asked Dolly, smartly. "If it is, I must say I think those stores you wouldn't stop at are much nicer!"

Holmes laughed back at her. He seemed to have taken a great fancy to her, spoiled and pert though she was.

"No, indeed," he said, "but I happened to see by that blue sign that they have a telephone inside, and I just remembered, after we passed through that last village, that I ought to telephone a message to a friend of mine in the city. So, if you don't mind, I'll leave you in the car while I run in and telephone. It won't take me a minute, and then we'll be on our way again."

Then he got out, and cutting off the motor, stepped into the store. In a moment Bessie was ready to take advantage of the opporunity that chance and his carelessness offered her.

"You keep perfectly still, Dolly," she said, earnestly. "I know it isn't supposed to be nice to listen to what you're not meant to hear, but I think this is a time when I've got a right to try to find out what I can. I may not be able to do it at all, but I'm going to do my best to listen to Mr. Holmes while he's sending that message and find out all I can about it. Do you see that window at the side of the store? Well, there's just a chance, I believe, that the telephone inside

may be near the window. If it is, I may be able
to find out what he's doing."

And, without giving Dolly a chance to protest,
or even to voice her surprise, Bessie slipped from
the car and ran lightly to the side of the ram-
shackle old building that served as a store.
Crouching down there, she was able to hear what
Holmes, inside, was saying, as she had hoped.
And the very first words she heard sent a thrill
through her, and banished any lingering regrets
she might have had at playing the part, usually
so dishonorable, of eavesdropper.

"Hello! Hello!" she heard him saying.
"What's the matter, Central? I want Hedgeville—number eight, ring five. Can't you get
that?"

Bessie did not know the number, but very few
people in Hedgeville had a telephone, and that
in itself was suspicious. She waited while
Holmes, expressing his impatience volubly, amid
sympathetic chuckles from the audience inside
the store, got his connection.

"Hello! Hello! Is that you, Weeks?" she heard him say, at last, and it was all she could do, when she heard the name of the man who had proved himself such a determined enemy to Zara and herself, to keep from betraying herself with a cry. "Yes, yes, this is Holmes! Where am I? Oh, ten miles from nowhere! You wouldn't know the place if I were to tell you. What you want to know is where I'm going to be an hour from now. What? Tell you? Well, that's what I'm trying to do! Listen a little and don't ask so many questions. I'm going to be in an automobile at Jericho. Know where that is?"

He waited, evidently listening to Weeks.

"Yes, that's right. You'll be there, eh? You've got the papers? Well, don't leave them at home. We don't want any mistake about this. I had a lot of luck, didn't expect to be able to do it so soon, or so easily. I'll tell you about that later. Jericho, then. You won't be late? And an hour from now. This is risky work, Weeks. If you make any of your fool breaks this time, you'll hear from me. Well, good-bye!"

As he said good-bye Bessie slipped back to
the automobile, and when Holmes came out, all
bluff good-nature, only Bessie's heightened color
showed that anything out of the ordinary had
happened to her. As soon as she returned, Dolly
began to hurl question after question at her, but
Bessie refused to answer.

"Keep quiet, Dolly!" she urged. "I'll tell
you all about it when I can, but this isn't the
time to talk. You don't want to let Mr. Holmes
know what I was doing, do you? Well, please
keep quiet, then!"

Of course, if Holmes planned to do anything
wrong, he would not have revealed his plans
boldly to the loafers in the store who had been
listening to his telephone conversation. Bessie
understood that what he had said probably meant
more to Farmer Weeks than it could to her or
any casual listener. But, even so, there was
plenty to disturb her in what she had heard.
Evidently the danger point was Jericho, and she

tried hard to remember what she had ever heard about that place. It was a little town, she thought, not far from Hedgeville—and, then, suddenly, she got a clue to the whole plot. She realized why the change in their direction had worried her. They were going toward Hedgeville, back toward the section of the country from which she and Zara had escaped with so much difficulty on account of Farmer Weeks's vindictive pursuit.

And she remembered, too, Charlie Jamieson's warning about crossing the state line. That, then, was what Holmes meant to do—get her into the state where, although she did not understand exactly how, she was in danger of being deprived of her liberty for a time at least. It would be easy enough, in the automobile. State lines are not well marked along country roads. Even now she might have crossed that imaginary boundary that spelled the difference between safety and peril for her.

"Listen to me, Dolly," she whispered, when

she had finished revolving her thoughts. "I
don't know what's going to happen, but I'm sure
that Mr. Holmes is trying to get me back to the
people I had to run away from in Hedgeville.
You remember—you know what happened when
we were on our way to General Seeley's place,
when that man caught Zara and carried her off?"

Dolly nodded, greatly excited.

"So you can see that I may get into a lot of
trouble, Dolly. You'll help me, won't you?"

"Of course I will! And I'm awfully sorry for
getting you into it in the first place, Bessie."

"Don't worry about that! I'm going to forget about it. But now remember that you must
do just as I say for the next hour or so, even if
you don't understand why. I don't know yet
what Mr. Holmes is going to do, and so I can't
make any plans ahead. I'll just have to try to
do the best I can to fool him when he shows his
hand, and it may be that the only way I can do
it is with your help."

"I'll help you, Bessie. I won't be silly again."

CHAPTER XI

A DARING MOVE

For some time, then, Holmes drove the car in what Bessie soon saw to be an aimless fashion. The morning was nearly done, and Bessie, used to guessing at the time from the sun, knew that it was very near noon. Holmes seemed to be doubling on his tracks, and to be driving in what resembled a circle, as if he were chasing his own tail, and at last Bessie determined to speak to him and try to make him show his hand. The suspense of waiting for something to happen was making her nervous. She felt that even the realization of her fears would be welcome, since then, at least, she could do something.

"Mr. Holmes," she said, "I really think you'd better be taking us back. It's very late, and I'm afraid Miss Mercer will be worried about us."

"Not she!" said Holmes, cheerfully. "The

fact is, I've rather lost my way, and those stupid men at that store where we stopped did not seem to be able to do much toward setting me right. So, knowing that we might be late, I took the liberty of telephoning to Miss Mercer and said that, if she didn't mind, I'd take you two to luncheon somewhere and bring you back in the afternoon.''

Bessie gasped at the cool daring of the way in which he told the lie. But then she reflected, just in time to keep her from taxing him with having told an untruth, that he knew nothing of her eavesdropping, and therefore thought it was safe to tell her anything he liked.

"Oh!' she said. "I—I didn't know you'd done that. You said you were going to send a message to a friend—''

"Well, I flatter myself that Miss Mercer and I are friends,'' said Holmes, smiling. "Why don't you cheer up, Miss Bessie? It's all right— really it is! You ought to know that I wouldn't get you into trouble with Miss Mercer for the world. Why, I'm old enough to be your father!"

"But if you're lost, how do you know where you're going?" asked Bessie, sticking to her guns.

"I don't know, of course—not exactly, that is. But I know that if I keep on going this way I'll come to some place where we can get a nice luncheon. This is pretty thickly settled country around here, you know, and it's used a lot by automobile parties. So we're sure to find some sort of a place soon. They have them wherever they think they can persuade motorists to stop and spend their money."

"If Miss Mercer knows where we are and said it was all right for us to stay it must be all right, Bessie, mustn't it?" asked Dolly, who had overheard what they were saying. "Oh, I'm so glad, Bessie! That shows you were mistaken, doesn't it, and that it wasn't so wicked of me to get you to come?"

"Hush, Dolly!" said Bessie, in a whisper. "I

can't let Mr. Holmes know it now, of course, but don't you remember that I heard him while he was telephoning, when he thought I was safe here in the car, and out of sight and sound of him? He didn't telephone to Miss Mercer at all. He's just saying he did, because he thinks he can fool me and make me believe anything he says. I heard what he telephoned, and he never even called up the farm!''

Even Dolly was a little scared at that. It never occurred to her to doubt what Bessie said. Somehow, people seemed always to be ready to believe her. And, remembering the way Holmes had declared that he had spoken with Miss Mercer, Dolly began to realize that Bessie was right, and that there must be something underhanded about Holmes. Bessie, although she was sorry that Dolly had to be frightened in such a fashion, was glad of the fact just the same, because it meant that she could depend upon Dolly now to obey her, no matter what she told her to do.

As a matter of fact, it seemed to Bessie that fear was about the only thing that did drive Dolly, who, if she thought the consequence would not be too unpleasant, usually managed to have her own way as decidedly as she had done in regard to accepting the offer of Holmes to take them to a place where they could get her much coveted ice-cream soda.

Bessie, remembering what she had heard Holmes say about meeting Farmer Weeks in an hour, began now to keep her eyes open, and she soon discovered that they had ceased their aimless driving about, and were traveling along what was evidently a highroad, since it showed the marks of many wheels and hoofs. And a glance at the sun was enough, too, to let her know that the crisis of this silly adventure was approaching, since nearly an hour had elapsed since she had overheard the conversation.

And, sure enough, just as she had expected, it was not long before Bessie saw that the houses along the road were closer and closer to one another, and a few moments later the tall, white steeple of a church and the smoke from the chimneys of a small town made it plain that they were approaching a town—most likely Jericho.

"Well, well, I know this place," said Holmes, turning to speak to them. "It's Jericho, and it's in your own state, Miss Bessie. Didn't you tell me that you used to live in Hedgeville? That's not so very far from here."

There was a strange look in his eyes as he looked fixedly at Bessie, and now she no longer had any doubt that he meant mischief, and that it behooved her, if she wanted to escape from the trap into which she was being led, to have all her wits about her. As they entered the town she kept her eyes open, but there was no sign of Farmer Weeks. He was late, and Bessie was glad of that, since, now that she could guess what she must face, every added minute of safety and freedom from interference was so much clear gain. A plan was forming in her head, a wild, reckless sort of plan, but still one that offered some chance, at least, of getting out of a very disagreeable position.

"Hungry?" asked Holmes, turning to them as he slowed the car near the railroad station. "Well, we'll have some lunch in just a minute. I'm just going in here to make some inquiries about the roads and I'll be right back."

Bessie's eyes followed him into the station, and then, just as she had done before, she slipped from the car as soon as he was inside, following him cautiously, but feeling that there was less danger than there had been at the store, since here, if she were surprised, she could explain that she felt cramped from the long ride, and had gotten out of the car to restore her circulation. Then, peeping inside, she saw Holmes talking eagerly, and, as she thought, angrily, to Jake Hoover!

"He'll be here soon—jes' as soon as he can get here," she heard Jake say. And she heard Holmes's angry reply, and nothing more, since

that was enough, and more than enough, to con-
firm her fears and make her understand that if
she was to get out of this trap she must make
a move at once. And now, knowing perfectly well
the risk she was running, she sped back to the
car, and climbed aboard, but in the front seat,
where Holmes had been sitting, and not next to
Dolly, in her own proper place. For her plan
was nothing more nor less than to get away in
Holmes's own car!

Bessie had never driven an automobile in her
life, and she knew as little, almost, as it was possible for anyone to know about them. But she
felt that all the sacrifices she had endured so far
would be made useless unless she got away, and,
moreover, she was sure now that Zara would need
her help more than ever. And if she could only
get a little distance away from Holmes, she was
sure that she and Dolly would be able to elude
him. So, doing exactly what she had seen Holmes
do, she threw in the clutch, and, with nervous,
trembling hands on the wheel of the big car,

guided it as it gathered speed and moved across the railroad tracks.

From the moment when the idea of making her escape in this fashion had first entered her mind, Bessie had watched Holmes and every move he made like a cat, determined to be able to do as he did if the emergency arose. And now her remarkable ability to do things that required the skilled use of her hands stood her in good stead.

The car was a silent one at low speed, and it had gone nearly a hundred feet before Holmes realized that something was wrong, and came running out of the station, followed by the wide-eyed Jake Hoover. And Bessie increased her start while he stood there, too stunned with amazement even to cry out.

By the time he had gathered his wits enough to begin shouting and running after his car, pursuit was hopeless, and Bessie, afraid any minute of having an accident, was running the car, still slowly, but too fast for anything but another car

to overtake it, out along the road that led out of
Jericho.

Dolly had screamed when she saw what Bessie
meant to do, but after that she had been too
frightened even to speak. But when they were
out of range of Holmes's shouts and angry cries
she regained her courage enough to lean over and
speak to Bessie.

"Oh, Bessie, do stop!" she begged. "We might
run into someone, or be run into ourselves. This
is awfully dangerous, I know!"

"So do I know that," said Bessie. "But we
had to do something, Dolly, and this was the only
thing I could think of to do, though I didn't want
to. But we're not going to stay in the car, don't
worry! Do you see that lane that comes into
the road just beyond that big oak tree? Well,
I'm going to turn up there, and leave the car so
that they can find it. I don't want to steal the
car, you know."

Bessie managed the turn successfully, and,
frightened as she was, even the few minutes that

she had spent in driving the car had thrilled and
exhilarated her. She ran slowly up the lane, and
when the main road was hidden by a curve, she
stopped the car and got out.

"There!" she said. "Dolly, if I only knew
more about running it, I'd like to go back to the
farm in the car. It would serve Mr. Holmes
right if we did, you know, for he was trying to
play a mighty mean trick on me. I wonder if
I'll ever be able to learn to drive a car like that?
I'd love to be able to, and to have one of my own
to drive!"

"How are we going to get home?" wailed
poor Dolly. "Oh, Bessie, what an awful fool
I've been! And now I'm hungry and tired, and
we're lost, and miles from the farm, and Miss
Eleanor will be furious at me!"

"Cheer up, Dolly! We'll get home all right.
And I'll see that Miss Eleanor understands all
right. She won't be angry. She'll probably tell
you that you've been punished enough when we
get back. I don't know about getting anything

to eat, though. We can't do that around here. All we want to do now is to get away from here."

Then suddenly she had an idea.

"I'm not going to steal his nasty old car," said Bessie, "but I am going to borrow something that ought to be in it, and that's a map! Anyone who travels around as much as he does must have maps that show the roads, and, as long as he has got us into this mess, I don't see why we shouldn't take something from his car to help us out of it. I'll send it back to him as soon as we get to the farm. Here—let's see—yes, here's a whole lot of little maps."

"Let me see, Bessie. I've seen those maps before. I bet I can find the right one that we want in a jiffy. Yes, here it is!"

"All right. Let's get off in the woods here and look at it, Dolly. We don't want to stay near the car, because they'll soon find that we turned up this lane, and they'll come looking for the machine and for us. So we want to be off where they can't see us. I'd hate to be caught again right now after taking such a chance with that automobile!''

"But you didn't act as if you were taking a chance, Bessie. I thought you were the bravest girl I'd ever seen—''

"Nonsense, Dolly! I was just as frightened as you were—more frightened, I guess. I didn't know whether what I was doing was right or not, and I was afraid every second I'd push the wrong thing, or touch something with my foot, and start it going as fast as it could.''

"Well, when I'm frightened, I show it, and I don't do things that I'm afraid of. Someone told me once that to do something you were really afraid to do was really the bravest thing— braver than if you're not afraid when other people would be.''

"Well, I was afraid, and the only reason I started that car was because I was more afraid to stay there than to run the car, Dolly. So I guess we needn't worry much about my having been brave. It was simply a question of which I

was the most afraid of—the car or Mr. Holmes.
Here, this is a nice spot. We can sit down on
this old log, and there's enough sunlight coming
down through the trees for us to see the map.''

They sat down together on the trunk of a fallen
tree, and put their heads together over the map.

"Here's Jericho, and here, see, Dolly, that's
the railroad we crossed. Here's the road—and,
yes, here's the lane we came up. It's a good
thing we didn't try to go much further, isn't it?
That star at the end means that it stops and just
runs into the woods. I expect they use it for
bringing out the trees after they're cut in the
winter.''

"Well, I'm glad we know just where we are,
but how are we going to get back, Bessie? That's
the chief thing, it seems to me. Don't you think
so?''

"I've got a little money with me,'' said Bessie, thoughtfully. "If we can walk until we get
to a railroad station—not the one at Jericho, of
course,—I think we ought to be able to get back

that way very easily. Let's look up Deer Crossing and see if that railroad doesn't run near here
somewhere.''

Bessie took the map then, and she found that
Jericho was in the same state as Hedgeville, just
as she had suspected. She did not know what
the Hoovers had done, and whether they had ob-
tained any papers giving them control of her, as
Farmer Weeks had done in the case of Zara, but
she was pretty sure that if she were caught in
their state Farmer Weeks would find some way
of keeping her there, and of preventing her from
getting back to Miss Mercer and her friends of
the Camp Fire Girls.

"Mr. Holmes took an awful roundabout way
to get here, Dolly," said Bessie, when she had
finished looking at the map. "But he didn't
really bring us so very far away. If we were
riding in an automobile, I don't think it would
take us more than an hour to get back. But, as
we haven't got a car, here's the best thing for us
to do. We can follow this lane, except that we'd

better walk through the woods instead of going back to the lane, and come out on another main road about two miles away. That will take us over here''—she pointed to a place on the map—''and there we can get a trolley car to this station. There'll be a train to take us to Deer Crossing from there, and then we can get home easily. Of course, we don't know how the trains run, and we may have to wait a long time for one, but it's the best thing to do, I'm sure.''

''Well, we'd better start right away, I guess,'' said Dolly, stoutly. ''I'm an awfully slow walker in the woods, Bessie. I'm not used to them. But I'll hurry as much as ever I can for I've given you trouble enough already to-day.''

The woods were very quiet, and Bessie was rather surprised at the absence of signs of life—human life, that is. Of squirrels and chipmunks and birds there were plenty, but it seemed strange to her that in so thickly settled a part of the country so much land should be left covered with woods. But it was good for their purpose, since she was sure that Holmes would have complained that his car was stolen, and he would not, of course, have told people the reason for Bessie's seemingly mad action. Nor would their word be likely to be taken against his. So the thing for them to do was to escape observation. And until just before the woods began to clear, they seemed likely to do so. But then there was a shock for Bessie, for, right in front, she suddenly heard Jake Hoover's voice.

CHAPTER XII

FRIENDS IN NEED

Bessie clutched Dolly's arm and drew her back just in time, for Dolly, growing enthusiastic at the sight of the road, had been about to spring forward with a cry of joy.

"That's Jake Hoover, the boy who used to bully me and tried to frighten us when we were all in camp. Do you remember, Dolly? We mustn't let him see us! He's in with Mr. Holmes and Farmer Weeks, and I'm really more afraid of him than I am of Mr. Holmes. He hates me, anyhow, and he'd do anything he could to hurt me, I believe."

They crouched down behind some bushes then, and worked their way forward cautiously, making as little noise as possible, until they could see the road and so have a chance to find out what Jake was doing in that neighborhood. At first

Bessie, who was in the van, did not see Jake, and, looking hastily up and down, she found that there were no houses in sight and that they had struck a lonely and solitary part of the road. Then she heard Jake's voice again, and, answering him, Mr. Holmes's.

"It's like looking for a needle in a haystack," growled Holmes. "If old Weeks had got to Jericho on time, we'd have saved all this trouble."

"He was doing his best, mister," said Jake. "But he had to take the train. He can't ride a bicycle, like me, and a horse and buggy would have taken him a long time. The old man done his best. 'Tweren't his fault he was late."

"Well, no use crying over spilt milk," said Holmes. "You'd better walk down this road until you come to the trolley line. Watch that. I think they'll try to get aboard the car there and get to the railroad that way. That would get them back to Deer Crossing, you see. Once they're out of this state, we can't touch Bessie, and the little baggage knows it. She's too clever for her own good. If they had been coming out this way they would be here by now, I think. But I had an idea they'd strike through the woods. They wouldn't follow the lane where they left my car, because they would know very well that we'd be watching that.''

"An' Bessie can find her way through any woods you ever seen," said Jake Hoover, gloomily. "Used ter run away from maw at home that-away, an' we never could find her till she got good an' ready to come home an' take her lickin'.''

Dolly grinned at Bessie.

"Good for you!" she whispered. "Did you really do that, Bessie? You're a good sport, after all! I never thought you'd be disobedient.''

Bessie smiled.

"Listen!" she whispered. "We mustn't talk yet.''

"What'll I do if they come to the trolley line?" asked Jake.

"Catch Bessie and hold her," said Holmes.

"Don't pay any attention to the other one, of course. We've nothing to do with her, and we don't want to be bothered by her. She's a silly, brainless little thing, anyway."

Bessie's hand sought Dolly's and held it tight. And Bessie, looking at her chum's face, saw that it was red with anger and mortification. It was a harsh blow to Dolly's pride in herself, and her belief in her own power to charm everyone she saw.

"Never mind, Dolly! You're not what he calls you, and we both know it," whispered Bessie. "Don't get angry! Remember that he's furious because we slipped out of his hands, that's all. I don't believe he really means that at all. He isn't silly enough to believe it, I'm sure of that."

"I bet I'll make him feel sorry he ever said that, just the same," vowed Dolly, clenching her fist. "I'd like to pull his hair out for him, the nasty, mean liar!"

"Well, we've got to think of getting away from

them before we can do that,'' said Bessie. ''And it's not going to be as easy as I thought, either, Dolly, because if they watch that trolley line, I don't see how we're going to get aboard without being seen. Jake Hoover is going down this road, you see.''

''Well, why don't we just strike the trolley at another place?''

''That isn't so easy, either, Dolly, because that trolley doesn't run along the road there. It goes through the fields, like a regular railroad, and it only stops at certain places. There isn't a trolley station marked for a mile or so either side of the one on this road, and I don't see how we can get to the nearest ones, either. I don't know the country around here well enough to do much wandering in the woods. You have to know your way about to do that, especially if you're in a hurry to get anywhere.''

''Sh—listen!'' said Dolly, holding up her finger.

''Well, you understand, then?'' said Holmes,

in the road below. "Take this road until you
come to the trolley line, and wait there for the
girls to come along. If Bessie comes, grab her,
and don't let her get away from you. I'll go to
the railroad station where they'll have to change
for the train to Deer Crossing, in case they manage
to reach it in some other fashion, and old Weeks
will stay on guard in Jericho. Now, don't make
any mistakes. Remember, I know some things
about you that you don't want others to find out,
young man, and I've got a habit of punishing
people who fail when they are working for me."

"I ain't noticed that you reward them much
when they do things," grumbled Jake. "It's a
poor rule that don't work both ways, mister. You
say you'll punish me if I don't make good; how
about payin' me if I do?"

"We'll talk about that when you've accom-
plished something, my young friend," said
Holmes, with an ugly laugh. "It seems to me
that you ought to be pretty grateful to me for
not having split on you before this, though. If

I told all I know about you, I guess you'd be in
the state reformatory now—and I'm not sure
that it wouldn't be a good place for you. Eh?''

"Stow that, you!" snarled Jake. "Say, I
could tell a few things about you if I wanted to.
This stunt you pulled off this morning is pretty
nigh to bein' kidnappin'—know that?''

Bessie touched Dolly on the arm.

"Oh, I do hope they keep on quarreling," she
whispered. "That is our very best chance to
escape from them, Dolly. If they get to fighting
between themselves, it's going to be much harder
for them to do anything to us. They'll distrust
one another, and we may be able to fool them.''

But Holmes evidently saw that, too. When he
spoke again, his voice was good-natured, and he
had resumed his chaffing, easy tone.

"Don't go up in the air that way, Jake," he
said. "I was only trying to string you a little,
trying to make you mad. I wouldn't give you
away; never fear that. You'll do your best, I
know. And you'll find that you'll get your re-

2—C13

ward, all right, too, if you make a good job of
this. We've got one of them. Now we want the
other, and I'll feel safe. So go ahead now and
don't waste any more time. Take your bicycle
and make the best time you can to that trolley
station.''

"I got a right to hold her, haven't I?" asked
Jake, a little dubiously, as Bessie thought.

"Sure you have!" said Holmes, impatiently.
"I've told you that, haven't I? Weeks has got
papers from the court making him her guardian,
just as he did in the case of that other girl."

"All right," said Jake.

And he got on his bicycle and rode off, while
Holmes walked back along the road, and they
heard him, a minute later, cranking up his automobile, which he had evidently found and taken
around by another road.

The information, unintentionally given to her
by Holmes, that Weeks was her legal guardian,
made Bessie shiver. She was more afraid of the
miserly old farmer than of anyone she had ever

seen, and the idea of being subject to his authority for any length of time filled Bessie with
dread. He hated her already; she knew that she
would be far less happy in his care than she had
ever been at the Hoovers', where, sometimes, it
had seemed to her that the limit of discomfort
and severe treatment had been reached.

So, if Bessie had needed anything to spur her
determination to escape from the trap into which
poor Dolly had so innocently led her, this acci-
dental discovery of what her fate was to be
would have been enough. But as she pondered,
she could not, for the time, see what was to be
done.

"Bessie," said Dolly, when they had been quiet
for several minutes, "is that Jake Hoover as
stupid as he looks?"

"He's not very bright, Dolly. He's cunning,
like some animals, and that makes him seem
cleverer than he is. But I think that he really
just acts by instinct most of the time, and that
that's one reason he's so mean."

"Well, have you thought of any way of getting back to the farm except by the trolley?"

"No—o. The only thing I did think of was that you might go ahead. They wouldn't bother you, I guess. They'd be afraid to, you see, because you've got a lot of friends and relatives who'd make an awful fuss if they tried to bother you. Then I could stay here, and you could tell Miss Eleanor, and she'd get Charlie Jamieson, or someone to come after me here in an automobile—"

"I think that's too risky, Bessie. They'd guess that I knew where you were, and if they're ready to take such big chances to get hold of you, they might carry me off and keep me somewhere for a few days—long enough to keep me from taking word to Miss Eleanor and bringing help to you. And you see you wouldn't know why they didn't come, and, oh, no, I think we'd better not try anything like that!"

"It would be risky, Dolly, and I know it as well as you do. But I don't see what else we're going to do. I hate to get you mixed up with my troubles—it isn't fair. I think I'd better just let them catch me, and take a chance of getting away afterward—"

"Bessie King, do you think I'd let you do anything like that? Whose fault is it that you're in this trouble? Mine, isn't it? Well, we're going to stick together! I'm certainly not going to let you get into more trouble just for the sake of saving me from sharing it. And I've got an idea, anyhow. Jake Hoover looks to me as if one could fool him pretty easily. He doesn't know what I look like, does he?"

"I don't suppose he does, Dolly. I don't see how he could. But what's that got to do with it?"

"Just you wait and see! If you had any plan, Bessie, I wouldn't want to suggest anything, because I think you're a lot cleverer than I am. But I have fooled boys before now, just for fun, and I think maybe I can do it this time, when I've really got a good reason for doing it.

These woods along the road here aren't very thick
so let's walk along, and follow the road, until we
come in sight of the trolley. Then we'll see what
it's like where the trolley comes along, and maybe we'll be able to fool Mr. Jake Hoover, the
horrid thing! I think he must be a dreadful
coward to persecute a girl the way he does you.
You never did anything to him, did you?''

"No, but he never liked me from the time he
was a little boy. He was always trying to get
me into trouble with Maw Hoover. I don't know
why he hates me so, but he certainly does.''

"Well, he doesn't hate you half as much as
I hate him, I promise you that, Bessie! And
I've usually managed to get even with the
people I hate, if it wasn't too much trouble. I'm
hungry now, and thirsty, and it's his fault—
partly. I'm going to get even with him for
that.''

Bessie was surprised to find that Dolly seemed
to have conquered her nervousness and her fear
of the strange situation in which she was placed.

A little while before she had seemed almost on
the verge of a collapse, and Bessie had been
afraid that her chum, unused to hardships of any
sort, and to roughing it, as country girls almost
all learn to do from the time they are very small,
was going to break down. But now Dolly seemed
to be as resolute and as unafraid as Bessie herself, and the knowledge naturally cheered Bessie,
since it assured her that she would not have to
bear the burden alone.

So they started, as Dolly had suggested, walking along through the woods, perhaps a hundred
feet back from the road. They could not be seen
themselves, but, by moving to the side of the little rise or bank along the road from time to time,
they were able to see what was going on. For
most of the distance they were unable to see anything at all. The road seemed to be little used,
and they passed only one house on the way to
the trolley station.

They had warning of their approach to the
trolley some time before it was in sight, too,

when they heard the wires singing as a car passed along.

"Now we're getting near the place," said Dolly, happily. "Oh, but it's going to be fun, Bessie! You're just going to let me run things now for a little while, for a change. I've got a splendid plan—and I'll tell you about it in good time."

As they neared the trolley line the woods began to get somewhat thinner, and Dolly grew nervous.

"I hope the ground isn't too clear around the track, Bessie," she said. "That wouldn't be good for my plan at all."

But her fears were groundless, for, as it turned out, the trolley line ran right through the woods on their side of the road, although on the other side the trees had all been cleared away. Soon they saw a little shed, and a bench outside. And on the bench, watching the road in the direction from which they had come, sat Jake Hoover.

"Now, listen," said Dolly. "Jake doesn't know me, you see, and I'm going right out there and talk to him. I bet he'll be glad to talk to me, too, and I'll keep him busy, so that you can sneak over the tracks and get to the other side. Then you wait there until you hear a car coming. See? And when it comes, get on from the other side. I'll be holding Jake's attention, and I don't believe he'll ever see you at all. I'll get aboard, too, and you can manage so that he won't be able to see you on the car. Even if he does, I don't believe the men would let him touch you, but he won't, until the car begins to move, and then it will be too late."

"But, Dolly, do you think you can keep Jake Hoover quiet? Suppose he knows you, he'd suspect right away that I was in the neighborhood. And then there's another thing. Mr. Holmes may have told him what sort of clothes you are wearing."

"I never thought of that, Bessie. That's so. Oh, I know! You change dresses with me, right here. He's so stupid that he'd never think of our doing that, I know.''

"That's a good idea, Dolly. I do think it may work.''

So, in the shadow of the trees they changed dresses, and then, while Bessie advanced toward the track cautiously and as quietly as possible, with her training in the woods, Dolly went back, and appeared presently walking carelessly along toward the trolley station.

Jake looked at her suspiciously, and she smiled at him.

"Oh, hello!" she said, cheerily. "You waiting for a car, too? How soon does the next one come along?''

"About two minutes," said Jake. He was eyeing her clothes, and evidently suspected nothing after that scrutiny.

"That's good! I was afraid I'd miss that car. Oh, you're not going, are you? That's your bicycle, isn't it?''

"Naw, I'm not goin'—got to stay here. Say,

why don't you wait here and talk to a feller?"

"I might," smiled Dolly. The car was really coming—it rounded a curve just then, and came in, slowing up. Dolly saw Bessie get aboard, but Jake was looking at her. "No, I guess I can't," she said then. And she sprang aboard, just as the car moved off.

CHAPTER XIII

The two girls fell into one another's arms on the car, laughing almost hysterically as it moved away. Looking back, Dolly saw Jake Hoover, a stupid look in his round eyes, staring after them.

"Bessie! Let him see you!" she begged. "I want him to know how he was fooled! I bet he's just the sort of boy to go around saying what poor things girls are, and how little use he has for them!"

Bessie stood up on the back platform, and Jake saw her. The sight seemed to drive him frantic. They saw him waving his arms, and faintly heard his shrieks of anger as he saw his prey slipping away. But he was helpless, of course; there was no way in which he could chase the car, and he had sense enough, at least, to realize that.

"You're quite right about him, Dolly," said

205

Bessie, laughing so hard that there were tears in her eyes. "He always did go around saying that girls were no good and that he couldn't see why any of the fellows wanted to have anything to do with them!"

"He's the sort that always does, Bessie, and it's because the girls won't have anything to do with them. He was pleased enough when I started talking to him, and awfully bashful, too, just like a silly calf. That's all he really is, anyhow, Bessie. But it's a good thing he's as silly as he is, because he's so mean that if he were clever, he could make a frightful nuisance of himself."

"I think he'll have a bad time when Mr. Holmes and Farmer Weeks find out that he let us get away, Dolly. I don't know what sort of a hold they've got on him, but it was easy to tell there was something, from the way Mr. Holmes spoke."

"Yes, indeed! And Mr. Holmes meant just what he said when he threatened him, too. The only reason he pretended afterwards that he was

joking was so that Jake wouldn't be too frightened to do anything, don't you think so?"

"Yes, I do, Dolly. I wonder if Miss Eleanor
and Mr. Jamieson will believe that I was right
about Mr. Holmes now? They laughed at me before when I said that I wouldn't trust him, and
was so sure that he had something to do with
Zara's being carried off—"

"Why, what's that, Bessie? I hadn't heard
of that at all."

"Oh, I forgot! You don't know about that,
do you? Well, this is a good chance to tell
you."

So Bessie told Dolly something of the strange
and involved affair of Zara and her father, and
of Zara's mysterious disappearance from the
Mercer house in the middle of the night.

"I'll bet they fooled her, just the way Mr.
Holmes fooled me," said Dolly, excitedly. "He
looks so nice, and he's so smooth and clever,
and he talks to you as if he wanted to be your
best friend. I don't believe they carried her off.

I think they fooled her, so that she was willing to go with them.''

"That's just what I think, Dolly, and this business today makes me worry about her more than ever. I think we ought to try to get her away from them and back with us just as soon as we can.''

"I suppose they wanted you because you know too much,'' said Dolly, thoughtfully. "They probably thought that you would try to get Zara away from them.''

"I think there's more than that, though, Dolly,'' said Bessie, her eyes shining with excitement. "I don't know what it is, but I've just got a sort of funny feeling that they know something about me that I don't know, and that they don't want me or my real friends to find out. I'm going to be just as careful as I can be, anyhow. Have you got that map we took from the car? I want to see just where this car will take us.''

Dolly produced the map, and they bent their heads over it. No one on the car seemed to be pay-ing much attention to them. There were only two or three passengers, and Bessie thought they had not seen the manner in which they had boarded the car. But the conductor, coming around for fares, had noticed that there was something out of the ordinary about their presence. He was smiling broadly when he held out his hands for the fare.

"Gave that young feller the slip pretty neatly back there where you got aboard," he remarked. "Which of you was he after? Don't blame him much—pretty young ladies like you!"

"Oh, he's just a stupid boy! We didn't want him riding with us," said Dolly, "so we tried to make him think we weren't coming on this car, and then jumped aboard when it was too late for him to follow us."

"I saw you—I saw you," chuckled the conductor. "So did Hank. He's my motorman, and the best one on the line. That's why he started the car to goin' so quickly. Lots of excitement around this way this morning."

"How's that?" asked Bessie.

2—C14

"Oh, there was a city feller over to Jericho kickin' that a couple of girls had stolen his automobile. Me, I don't believe it—didn't like his looks. Serves him right, I say, if they did."

Bessie was afraid that Dolly would betray them by a laugh, but nothing of the sort happened. It was quite plain that the conductor never thought of connecting them with the two girls Holmes had charged with the theft of the car. But, even so, the knowledge that he had made such an accusation publicly worried Bessie. She did not know much of the law, and she was afraid that she and Dolly might possibly have rendered themselves liable to arrest by taking the car, even though they had abandoned it almost at once, and Holmes had recovered it undamaged.

In that case, she feared getting out of the state might not save them. They might, for all she knew, be arrested and taken back to Jericho, where she would be in the power of Weeks. However, she decided not to worry much about that,

and when she mentioned her fears, Dolly laughed
at them.

"People in glass houses can't afford to throw
stones," she said, sagely. "Look here, Bessie, he
might be able to make people believe that he had
a right to catch you, if he was acting for this
nasty old Farmer Weeks. But they haven't any
right to touch me, and I believe they could make
a lot of trouble for Mr. Holmes for carrying me
off. I remember that they sent a man to prison
for a long time not long ago for carrying off a
child that lived near us. I guess Mr. Holmes
won't be very anxious to go to law about his old
car."

"Well, look here, Dolly, we're not quite out of
the woods yet, you know. Here's the station
where we have to get out to catch the train for
Deer Crossing. It's marked Tecumseh. And it's
a funny thing, but the railroad is in the other
state, and the trolley car stops in this one. Do
you see? When we get off the car we'll still be in
this state, but it won't take more than a minute

to cross the line. Mr. Holmes told Jake he'd be waiting there, so we must look out."

"Oh, Bessie, are you sure? Wouldn't it be dreadful to have escaped this far, and then be caught just when everything seemed to be all right? I'd rather have been held up by Jake Hoover, I do believe! And I thought everything was all right now."

"Well, there's no use getting discouraged. We're much better off than we were when we were in the car, Dolly, and we got out of that mess. So we might as well try to think that we'll be all right, anyhow. Oh, I just thought of something! Is there a station on this trolley line before we come to Tecumseh?"

They looked eagerly at the map, but disappointment was their lot. There was no station between the one where they had boarded the car and Tecumseh. But Dolly had an idea again, just as they had about decided that they would have to take their chances with Holmes at Tecumseh.

"Doesn't this car ever slow down at all between stations?" she asked the conductor, smiling
and looking as attractive as she could.

"Well, that depends," said the conductor, re-
turning the smile. "If a passenger's got a pull
with me or the motorman, it might. Why?"

"Because if we go to Tecumseh, we'll only have
to walk back nearly half a mile to that road that
crosses the track. Couldn't you let us off there,
Mr. Conductor?"

"Well, I don't run the car," he said, with a
smile. "But I'll talk to Hank, the motorman.
Never knew him to refuse anything a lady asked
yet."

He walked to the front of the car, and returned
a moment later.

"Hank says he's got to stop at that road today," he reported, with a grin. "It's against
the rules, you know, to make stops except at
stations, or to let passengers off. But the car
has to stop sometimes, just the same, and if you
should happen to drop off, I won't see you—I

won't be looking. You move back to the door, and be ready, and I'll stay up in front with Hank. Then I won't be to blame, you see, if you should happen to get off when the car stops."

"Thank you ever so much," said the two girls, together. "It's awfully good of you—"

"Don't be thanking me," grinned the conductor. "The car'll be stopping by accident like, and how should I know what you're going to do? Well, good luck to you!"

They had not long to wait before the grinding of the brakes warned them that the time was at hand, and in a few moments they stood beside the track and waved their hands cheerily to the conductor, who, with an expression of mock surprise on his face, had come out on the back platform, and pretended to wonder how they had got off the car.

"Now I think it ought to be easy," said Bessie, greatly relieved. "You see, Mr. Holmes will be watching the car. He probably knows all about this line, and wouldn't think of our being able

to get off and walk. So what we want to do
is to follow this road here and then turn east
at the first crossroads. That will bring us to
the railroad track, and we can cross it, and
work down to the station at Tecumseh, and be
safe all the way. We'll cross the state line
this side of the railroad, and then we'll be all
right.''

Dolly began to sing for sheer happiness.

"We're awfully lucky, Bessie," she cried.
"I'm ever so glad that things seem to be coming
out all right. If they'd caught you, I would always have blamed myself and thought it was
all my fault."

"Well, even if it was partly your fault in the
beginning, Dolly, I never would have got away
from Jake Hoover without you, I'm sure of that.
So you needn't worry any more."

"It's awfully good of you to say so, Bessie.
There's one thing—I'm not going to be silly any
more, the way I was about those ice-cream sodas
this morning. And I think—yes, I will—I'll

promise you right now not to have any soda or any candy between meals for a month. You think they're bad for me, don't you?"

"I think they must be, Dolly, or the Camp Fire Girls wouldn't give honor beads for doing without them. I've never had much of anything like that myself, you see, so I don't really know."

"Well, I won't take them, anyhow. Oh, Bessie, but I'm hungry! I'd give all the ice-cream sodas I ever ate for a big piece of beefsteak right now! Aren't you hungry, too? I should think you'd be starved."

"I am pretty hungry, but I was so excited I'd forgotten about it, I guess. Why did you remind me?"

"Well, maybe there'll be a store at Tecumseh, so that we can get something to eat."

"Here's the crossroad, Dolly. Now we want to turn east. I don't think we'll need to walk very far—three-quarters of a mile, maybe, and about as much more back toward Tecumseh when we're once beyond the railroad."

"I suppose it's safe to walk along the road here?"

"I think so, and the fields are open on both sides, anyhow, so it's a case of Hobson's choice. We'd be seen just as easily if we walked in the fields, and perhaps the people who own them would get after us, too. And I think we've got troubles enough on our hands without looking for any more."

"That's certainly true, Bessie. Yes, we'll have to stick to the road. Anyhow, we left Jake back at the trolley station, and he's probably still there, trying to puzzle out how we got away. And Mr. Holmes ought to be at Tecumseh. Farmer Weeks was to stay in Jericho, so I think we've really found a safe road at last!"

It seemed so, certainly. They met a few people and they were mostly driving, and Bessie was hoping for a ride. But everyone they met seemed to be going in the opposite direction, and they had crossed the railroad tracks before a cart finally overtook them. By that time, of course, they were ready to turn and follow the tracks to Tecumseh, so the cheerful offer of a ride from the farmer who was driving had to be declined.

"Oh, Dolly, we're really safe at last!" exclaimed Bessie. "They can't touch me in this state so we can sit down and rest if we want to."

"But I don't want to, Bessie. I'd rather hurry along to Tecumseh and get a train just as soon as we can. Wouldn't you? I think Miss Eleanor must be awfully worried about us by this time."

"Bessie!" said Dolly, suddenly. "Look, isn't that cloud of dust on the road there coming this way? It looks like someone on a bicycle."

It was. It was Jake Hoover, scorching along toward them, and as he approached them they could see a look of triumph on his face. He was up with them in a moment, and, jumping off his wheel, seized Bessie, who was too terrified to move.

"Got yer, ain't I?" he shouted, savagely exul-
tant. "Thought you was mighty smart, foolin'
me, didn't yer? Well, we'll see!"

"Don't you dare touch her! She's not in your
state any more," stormed Dolly, stamping her
foot.

"She soon will be," he said, and picked Bessie,
who was no match for him, though she struggled,
up in his arms. He started to walk back in the
direction he had come, leaving his bicycle in the
road where it had fallen.

But now Dolly, seeing Bessie treated so
roughly, seemed to turn into a little wildcat. With
a furious cry she sprang at Jake, and began hit-
ting him with her fists, scratching him, pulling
his hair and attacking him so vigorously that he
cried out with surprise and pain. He dropped
Bessie and turned to protect himself, and Dolly
drew off at once.

"Run, Bessie, run! He'll never catch you!"
she cried. And as Jake darted off in pursuit
of Bessie, who seized the chance to escape,

Dolly picked up a stone and smashed the bicycle with it.

"There, now! He'll never catch us on foot, and he can't ride any more," she cried. "Come on, Bessie!"

CHAPTER XIV

THE ENEMY CHECKMATED

Bessie had eluded the furious Jake easily enough. Amazed by Dolly's onslaught, he had been too surprised to move quickly in any case, and, when he saw her trying to ruin his bicycle, he was diverted from Bessie and, shouting furiously, ran toward her with the idea of saving his wheel. So it was no trick at all for the two girls, light on their feet and graceful in their movements, to avoid the shambling, ungainly, overgrown boy, who, smarting from the pain of the scratches Dolly had inflicted, ran after them blindly.

Moreover, they had not gone very far when a farmer's boy came along, driving a surrey. He was laughing at the antics of Jake, and when he saw the two girls, he stopped his horses.

"Say, is that big lout trying to catch you two?" he asked.

"He certainly is!" said Dolly. "Are you going to let him do it?"

"You bet your life I'm not!" said the boy, getting down from the surrey quickly. "Just you watch those horses, and you'll see what I do to him. We don't think much of fellers who hit girls in these parts."

Jake was coming along puffing and blowing, and when he saw the two girls he gave a cry of triumph. But the farmer's boy checked that quickly, and gave him something else to shout about.

"Here, you big bully, what are you trying to do?" he demanded, setting himself squarely in Jake's path.

"Get outer my way!" stormed Jake. "That young one there smashed my wheel, and the other one is wanted—she's wanted by the officers —she stole a automobile and set my pop's barn on fire—"

"That's a likely story—I don't think!" sneered the farmer's boy. "Get back now! Leave them alone, do you hear? If you try to touch them again, I'll knock you into the middle of next week—"

But Jake was too enraged to be afraid, as in his sober senses he certainly would have been. And rashly he made a quick leap forward, and tried to get out of the way of the big young fellow who was between him and the girls. There wasn't any fight; it would not be fair to dignify what followed with such a name. Jake was knocked down by the first blow; he tried to get up, and was promptly knocked down again. That brought him to his senses.

"Had enough?" asked his conqueror, simply.

And Jake, lying in the dust at his feet, sobbing, and trying to pull himself together, stammered out, "Yes!"

"All right! Get up, and go over there by the side of the road and sit down. And if you know what's good for you, you'll stay there, too, or else turn around and go where you came from. If you follow us you'll get into trouble—more than you're in now, and that seems to be about all you can handle, judging from the looks of you.''

Then he turned away contemptuously, and went back to Dolly and Bessie, who were watching him admiringly.

"Isn't he splendid—so brave and strong?" cried Dolly.

"It's a good thing for us he came along," said Bessie. "Jake is strong enough to hurt us or do anything he likes to us, but I always knew that he couldn't do anything against a boy his own size. I wish they hadn't had to fight, but in a case like this it's all right, because it's the only thing to do.''

"Well, I like a boy who can fight when he has to," said Dolly, stoutly. "I haven't any use for sissies, and I think that's all Jake really is, for all his bluster.''

"Well, I guess he won't bother you much more," said their champion, when he returned to the surrey. "I'm only going as far as Tecumseh,

but I'll be glad to give you a ride that far if you
want to go.''

"We do, indeed," said Bessie. "And we're
ever so much obliged to you for saving us from
that fellow and for offering us the ride, too. Do
you know when we can get a train at Tecumseh
for Deer Crossing?"

"Right soon now," said·the boy. "It's due
most any minute but I'll get you there in time.
That's the train I'm going to meet—got to take
some summer boarders from the city out to pop's
place. My name's Bill Burns. My pop's got a
farm over that way"—he pointed with his whip—
"about two miles."

Bessie and Dolly told him their names then, and
he asked where they were staying at Deer Crossing.

"Mercer Farm, huh?" he said, when they had
told him. "I got a cousin works over there—
fellow by the name of Walter Stubbs. Do you
know him?"

"Yes, indeed," said Bessie, with a smiling look
2—C15

at Dolly. "We saw him this morning. Dolly thinks a lot of him."

"Oh, is that so?" said Bill Burns. He looked at Dolly, then bent over and whispered to Bessie, "He's welcome to her." Then he spoke aloud again. "I may be running over to see Walt one of these days. He and I are pretty good friends —for cousins. Seems to me he told me somethin' about an ice-cream festival over there at the Methodist Church. I might run over to that."

"I wish you would," said Bessie, laughing. "All the girls are going, I'm sure—all our Camp Fire Girls."

"What, more of you girls?" said Bill, seeming to be surprised.

"Yes, indeed. There are a whole lot over at the farm. They'll be glad to see you, especially when we tell them how good you were to us, and how you saved us from that nasty Jake Hoover."

"Oh, I just enjoyed beating him," said Burns. "Wish he'd put up more of a fight, though. I'd have licked him just the same, but it would have

been more like a real fight. Well, I don't hear
that train yet, and the station's just around that
next bend. Not much of a place—Tecumseh.
Hasn't any right to such a fine name, I think.''

The prospect when they rounded the turn in the
road bore out his slur on the village of Tecumseh.
It wasn't much of a place—scarcely more than
the village part of Hedgeville, as Bessie saw. The
station was there, and two or three stores and a
post office. But Bessie and Dolly were more in-
terested in the man who was sitting gloomily,
watch in hand, on the station steps. It was
Holmes, and his face, when he saw them, was a
picture.

''Well, how in the world did you get here?''
he asked, angrily. ''That was a fine trick you
played on me, running off, and leaving me to
worry about you! You might have been
killed.''

''I like your nerve!'' exclaimed Dolly, before
Bessie could answer, surprised by the cool way in
which Holmes tried to shift the blame to their

shoulders. "Look here, Mr. Holmes, we know all about you, and why you took us on that ride. You wanted to get Bessie into the state where she came from, so that Farmer Weeks could keep her there!"

A look of black anger swept across his face, handsome enough when he did not let his real character stand revealed.

"Yes, there's no use trying to deceive us any more with your smooth talk, Mr. Holmes," said Bessie. "I listened to what you said over the telephone, and we heard you telling Jake Hoover how to catch us when we went to take the trolley, too."

"Yes," countered Dolly. "If you had been as smart as you thought you were, you could have caught us then—we were within a few feet of you while you were talking to him."

"Well, I'm near enough to catch you now!" said Holmes, and he made a grab for Bessie, and caught her just as she started to run away. He began dragging her across the tracks and toward

the state line, but Bill Burns came out of the post
office at that moment.

"Here, you let her alone!" he shouted, spring-
ing forward, and Holmes dropped Bessie's arm
to ward off the blow that Burns aimed at him.

"What are you butting in for?" he snarled.
"Want to get yourself in jail?"

"Never you mind what I want to do," said
Burns. "Don't you try to touch either of those
girls again! If you do, you'll find that I can hit
you as hard as you ever was hit in your life.
And if I ever get into jail, you won't be the one
to put me there, either—I'll bet money on that!"

There might have been more argument, but
just then the whistle of the approaching train
sounded, and a moment later it had drawn into
the station, separating the two girls and Burns
from Holmes very effectually.

Bessie and Dolly sprang up the steps at once,
and turned to wave good-bye to Bill Burns, who
had helped them so splendidly. He stood below,
grinning at them, and waving his hand, and as

they began to move out of range he called out
cheerily to them: "Well, I'll be over to see Walt
pretty soon. Don't forget what I look like!"

"We certainly won't," Bessie answered.

Then they went inside, and sank gratefully and
happily into the first empty seat they saw. They
were still hungry, but at least they were safe now
from the pursuit of Holmes and Jake Hoover,
and they were so grateful for that that they were
entirely willing to let their hunger be forgotten.

And they had not been seated more than a minute, when Bessie, at least, had new cause for feeling happy, for a man's voice sounded in her ear,
and she looked up in surprise to see Charlie
Jamieson, the lawyer, bending over them.

"Well, what are you doing here?" he exclaimed.

They told him as quickly as they could, both
girls joining in the story, and his eyes grew grave
as he listened.

"Well, I owe you an apology, Bessie," he said,
when they had finished their tale. "I certainly
thought you were all off about Holmes, and I'm

still puzzled to account for his being mixed up in this. But there's no doubt that he is, from what you tell me—none at all! He's a hard man to have to fight, too. You did mighty well to get rid of him as well as you did. You left him back there at Tecumseh, eh? Well, I'll just have a look, in case he got on the train when you weren't looking.''

He walked through the train, and in a few minutes he was back, looking more serious than ever.

''That's just what he did,'' he said. ''He's up there in the smoking car, looking as if he'd lost his last friend this morning. He's a hard man to shake off, and a bad man to have against you. That's always been his reputation, and I guess you two will be ready to believe that after what you've seen of him today. I'm going to sit down and do some thinking now, before we get to Deer Crossing. It's a lucky thing I happened to decide to run out this afternoon, and it was just accident. I found I had a little time to myself, and I wired to Miss Mercer that I would come out and spend the night and see how the Camp Fire Girls were getting along.''

I thought maybe she'd sent word to you when Dolly and I weren't at the farm for lunch,'' said Bessie. ''I'm afraid she's worried about us.''

''She probably is, and if she hadn't known I was coming anyhow she would probably have sent for me. Well, you'd better rest up a bit now, Bessie. We may not be through with Mr. Holmes yet.''

''He wouldn't dare try to do anything to me now, when you're here, Mr. Jamieson!''

''No, I don't believe he would. But that's not exactly what I meant. He's through with us— for the day. But we're not through with him. We may have a chance to get even and do something to him, just by way of a change. I think he needs a lesson to show him that we're a match for him, after all.'' Then he went off, explaining that he had to be alone to think out a problem.

But they hadn't figured out what his plan might

be when he returned to them, chuckling mightily.

"I've got it, I believe," he said. "Holmes acted as if you had treated him badly, didn't he, when you took his car? As if he was hurt by your thinking that he didn't mean to do just what he said?"

"Yes," said Bessie.

"Then we'll pretend to believe it, Miss Mercer and I. You needn't, of course. That wouldn't fool him for a minute. But he'll probably try to make us think he's all right, and that's just what I want. Oh, we've got him now, I think! I hope Miss Mercer will be at the station. I can't explain my plan now, but you'll be in it, and then you'll see. I'm going up to talk to him now."

So Bessie and Dolly, sadly puzzled, and unable to see what the lawyer was driving at, saw the two men get off the train at Deer Crossing. Jamieson rushed over to Miss Mercer and spoke to her for a minute, and then Eleanor, laughing, held out her hand to Holmes, and turned to the two girls with a smile.

"Why, how silly you were," she said, "to think that Mr. Holmes meant to be anything but kind! You mustn't get such nonsensical ideas. Mr. Holmes, just to prove that you don't bear any malice, you must let me drive you out to the farm for dinner. No, I really won't let you refuse. I insist. There's plenty of room in the car—the chauffeur will go back in one of the farm wagons, and Charlie will drive."

Holmes glanced once at Bessie triumphantly but he was careful not to betray himself.

"I'm afraid I oughtn't to impose on you, Miss Mercer," he said. "But really, since you're so pressing—well, I shall be most happy to come."

CHAPTER XV

When they arrived at the farm, after the swift run in the Mercer car, Miss Mercer took Holmes out on the big back piazza, and Bessie and Dolly, under the watchful eyes of Jamieson, made up for their long fast. It was nearly five o'clock in the afternoon when they reached the dining-room, and Jamieson laughed as he saw them eat.

"You'll spoil your appetites for dinner," he said, as he saw Dolly making away with the cold meat and bread and milk that had been provided for them.

"I don't care!" she answered. "It couldn't taste half as good as this, no matter what it was. But now you're not going to keep on being mean? You'll tell us why you and Miss Eleanor are being so nice to Mr. Holmes?"

"Not yet," he said. "But you'll know soon

enough. It isn't just because we like the pleasure of his company, I can tell you that. Mr. Holmes is in for one of the worst surprises of his life before I get through with him, unless I fall down pretty hard. And I don't expect to. I'll tell you one thing, though. All you girls are going for a straw ride tonight, and Mr. Holmes is going to be along, too. He doesn't know it yet, and he won't know, even after we start, just where we're going.''

''It's a lucky thing Miss Eleanor has taken part in amateur theatricals sometimes,'' he continued. ''She was half wild with anxiety about you two, and she was ready to give you the worst scolding you ever listened to. But I told her what I wanted her to do just in that one minute there at the station, and she played up splendidly, so that I don't believe Holmes suspects that we're on to him at all. She's mad with curiosity, too, and I bet she's dying to get hold of me and make me tell her all about it.

''Well, I've got to get ready for what's coming

after dinner. Run along upstairs, you two, and try to sleep for an hour or so."

"You won't leave us behind?" said Dolly, anxiously.

"I'd leave you in a minute, you minx, but I couldn't get Bessie without waking you up too, I suppose, and I need her, so you'll have to come along. If you see the other girls don't tell them what's happened. Make them wait until tomorrow."

"All right," said Bessie. "Come along, Dolly! I *am* tired. It will feel good to get a little nap."

The reaction from the strain of their experiences made it easy for them to get to sleep as soon as they were lying down, and both were still sleepy when a knock at the door awakened them. It was quite dark, and the moon was shining. Outside they found two wagons, one much larger than the other, filled with straw.

"This is fine fun," said Holmes, who was standing with Miss Mercer and Jamieson. "A regular old-fashioned straw ride, eh?"

"Well, pile in!" said Jamieson, who was acting as master of ceremonies. "Holmes, get in there beside Miss Mercer. Bessie, you and Dolly get in there, too. We want to keep an eye on you, so that you don't get into any more mischief. Come on, now, all you girls get aboard the other wagon—and off you go!"

Then he climbed aboard himself, and began to take up the song that had already been started in the other wagon, one of the favorites of the Camp Fire Girls. So it was a jolly party that soon passed out of the tree-lined avenue of the Mercer farm and began driving along the road, away from Deer Crossing.

The smaller and lighter wagon took the lead and they passed along quietly for some time— quietly as far as incident is concerned, that is, for there was nothing quiet about the merry, happy girls in the big wagon. They made the night resound with their songs and laughter, and Bessie wondered a little why she and Dolly were kept where they were, instead of being sent with the

other girls. But she said nothing, and she knew
that she would find out presently. For her and
Dolly there was a peculiar thrill in the ride, and a
delightful one, too, for they knew from what the
lawyer had told them that there was a surprise
preparing for Holmes, and it was exciting to try
to guess what it might turn out to be.

Nor was the explanation very long delayed.
They had driven for a mile, perhaps, when the
driver, obeying a quiet order from the lawyer, who had taken a seat beside him, turned
off the main road, and they found themselves
in a narrow lane, where there would not be
room to pass should they meet any sort of a
vehicle.

"Pretty narrow quarters, Jamieson," said
Holmes. "Are you sure you know where you're
going?"

"Yes, I know," said Jamieson, with a laugh.
"Don't you? I thought you knew this part of
the country so well, Holmes."

"I? No, I scarcely know it at all, as a matter

of fact. That's how I got lost this morning when
I took these young ladies for a drive and got myself into their bad graces.''

''My mistake! I thought you did know it.''

Jamieson bent over then and spoke again to
the driver, and in a moment they made another
turn, but this time into a private road. Bessie
thought she heard a startled exclamation from
Holmes, but she was not sure. Then she looked
around.

''What a horrid place!'' exclaimed Miss Mercer. ''Look how it's been allowed to run down.
Oh, I know where we are! This is the old Tis-
dall place. No one has lived here for years.
That's why it looks so neglected.''

''Right!'' said Jamieson. ''Doesn't that house
look creepy, through the trees, with the moonlight
on it? I thought this would be a fine place to come
and tell ghost stories.''

This time there was no mistake about Holmes's
angry exclamation.

''Look here, what do you think you're doing?

What right have you to bring this crowd in here, Jamieson?"

Charlie looked at him in surprise—a surprise that Bessie knew instinctively was assumed.

"Oh, strictly speaking, I suppose we're trespassing," he said. "But this has always been common property—for years, at least. The owners don't pay any attention to the place. They won't mind our coming here, even if they find out."

"Well, I object—"

But Holmes stifled the remark before anyone save Bessie and Jamieson heard it. And Bessie began to understand, and to thrill with a new, scarcely formed idea. She began to have a glimmering of Jamieson's plan, and she saw how cleverly Holmes had been induced to walk into the trap that had been set for him. No matter how much he knew about this mysterious place, and how unwilling he might be to let them explore it, whatever his reason, he could not protest now without revealing plainly that he had been lying

2—C16

before. And, moreover, he could not be at all sure that it was not pure accident that had led Jamieson to select it as their destination.

Holmes was between two fires. If he let the ride go on, he faced discovery of something he was trying to keep secret; if he tried to stop it short, or to divert it to some other spot, he was sure to arouse suspicions that, by the merest luck, as he supposed, his treatment of Bessie and Dolly had not aroused. So he did what most people would do in the same circumstances; he kept still, and trusted to his luck to carry him through.

"Oh, I see," he said, finally. "You're going to stop in the grounds and have a picnic, or something like that, eh? That's fine—that will be great sport."

"That's what I thought," said Charlie Jamieson, innocently, but Bessie was sure that he had winked at her.

The wagons drove up, however, to the very front of the crumbling old house.

"Everybody out!" called Jamieson. "Here,

Holmes, where are you going? Stay with us, man! The fun is just going to begin." For he had seen Holmes trying to slip off to the back of the house, and, smiling, he had seized the retired merchant's arm.

"Here's something I want you to hear," he said. "Eleanor, start the girls to singing that song I like so much—that 'Wohelo for Aye' song, you know."

In a moment the clear voices were raised in the most famous of all the Camp Fire Songs, and Holmes, with a savage wrench, got himself free. But it was too late. For, as the first notes rose, a window above was flung open, and a voice that Bessie knew as well as she did her own joined in the chorus. In a moment the singing stopped, and every pair of eyes was turned up, to see Zara leaning from a window!

"Oh, Bessie—Miss Mercer—please take me away from here! I'm so frightened!"

"The game's up, Holmes," said Jamieson, in a changed voice. "Did you really think we'd take your word against those two girls you treated so shamefully today? Come on, now, I'm not going to stand for any nonsense! Will you take me upstairs to where you've got Zara hidden? You played a cool game, and you thought you could get away with it because you were so respectable. But we've got a complete case against you. It was in your automobile that Zara was taken from Miss Mercer's house, and as soon as you played that trick today I was sure that you had had a hand in the game."

Holmes looked at him darkly. His face was working with anger, but he evidently saw that the game was up, as Jamieson said.

"I guess you win—this time," he said at last, coolly enough. "But remember, I haven't been beaten very often. And you don't know what's back of this. If you knew when you were well off, you'd keep out of this, Jamieson. There'd be something in it for you—"

"Don't try to bribe me," said Jamieson, with a gesture of disgust. "It's no use. I win, as you say. There may be a next time—but I'm not afraid of you, Holmes. Take me up there right away—"

"Oh, all right," said Holmes.

And three minutes later Zara was in Bessie's arms, while Holmes looked on, sneering.

"I'll not deny that you did a pretty clever job here," he said. "How did you find out about this house?"

"I happened to be searching some records yesterday, and I saw, quite by accident, the deed recording your purchase of this property," Jamieson answered. "That didn't mean much—until I heard of the way you acted to-day. Then, of course, I put two and two together, and decided you got hold of this place to keep Zara hidden.

"You knew there was a good chance that we could upset that order making old Weeks her guardian, and I knew, of course, that she hadn't been produced in court in the other state. Pretty risky work, Holmes. Now get out. You can stay here, of course, or you can walk to the station.

There won't be room for you with us, I'm sorry to say."

"Oh, I'm so glad to get away," Zara sobbed. "I thought it was best to go. They told me that I wouldn't be taken back to Farmer Weeks, and that my father wanted me to go with them. They had a note from him, and he said he didn't quite understand but that he was sure Mr. Holmes was his friend, and would look after me properly. And they said Bessie would be in danger as long as I stayed with her. That is really why I went."

"But it's all right now, Zara," Eleanor Mercer said, soothingly. "We'll look after you now. Didn't they treat you well here?"

"Oh, it was horrid, Miss Eleanor! They kept me locked up in that room, and I never saw anyone at all, except one old woman, who was deaf, and couldn't understand me. She brought my meals, but of course I couldn't talk to her."

"He was afraid to trust anyone she could talk to, of course, or who could answer questions if

anyone happened to come here. That explains
why the people inside didn't pay any attention
to all the noise we made as we drove up. That
was the one thing I was afraid of, and I couldn't
figure out any way to avoid that risk."

"But why did you bring Mr. Holmes along?"

"So that he wouldn't get here before we did
and get her away, Eleanor. That was why I
had to make him think we swallowed that ridic-
ulous story of his, too. Well, Dolly, will you
forgive me now for not telling you before?
Wasn't the surprise worth waiting for?"

"That—and getting Zara back. Of course it
was," said Dolly happily. "Oh, Zara, we're
going to have such good times on the farm now!"

"On the farm, yes," said Jamieson, dryly.
"But no straying into the road! And you'd
better see that half a dozen of them are always
together, Eleanor. Mr. Holmes isn't the sort to
be content with one licking. He'll come back for
more, or else I'm mightily mistaken in my man."

Then they all climbed into the wagons again,

and how they did laugh at the disconsolate figure of Mr. Holmes, whom they passed, trudging slowly and unhappily toward Deer Crossing.

Jamieson looked at his watch. Then he laughed merrily.

"He'll have to wait until half past five in the morning for the milk train to take him back to the city," he said. "I don't envy him. There isn't much to do at Deer Crossing."

www.ingramcontent.com/pod-product-compliance
Lightning Source LLC
Chambersburg PA
CBHW020758250626
47155CB00003B/1135